Cold Mountain

CHARLES FRAZIER

Level 5

Retold by Mary Tomalin
Series Editors: Andy Hopkins and Jocelyn Potter

Pearson Education Limited
Edinburgh Gate, Harlow,
Essex CM20 2JE, England
and Associated Companies throughout the world

ISBN 0582 81989 X

First published in Great Britain by Hodder and Stoughton 1997
This edition first published by Penguin Books 2004

Set in 11/14pt Bembo
Printed in Spain by Mateu Cromo, S.A.Pinto, Madrid

Produced for the Publishers by Bluestone Press, Charlbury, Oxfordshire, UK

Published by Pearson Education Limited in association with
Penguin Books Ltd., both companies being subsidiaries of Pearson Plc

For a complete list of the titles available in the Penguin Readers series please write to your local
Pearson Education office or to: Marketing Department, Penguin Longman Publishing,
Edinburgh Gate, Harlow, Essex CM20 2JE.

Contents

Introduction

Inman shaved in front of a metal mirror. The eyes that looked back at him had a look that he did not remember, a look that was more than just food hunger. It was a killer face, with eyes that looked at you sideways. But Inman tried to believe that this face was not him in any true way, and that it could in time be changed for a better one.

It is the period of the American Civil War (1861–65), and the northern states are winning the war against the southern states. A wounded soldier from the South has deserted from the army and is trying to return to his home in the Appalachian mountains and the woman he loves. The journey home is long and dangerous, and Inman does not know if he will return alive. The war has done terrible things to people, and he witnesses great poverty, cruelty, and violence. Can Inman save his soul, or will he turn into the animal that others have become?

Cold Mountain is a deeply poetic novel that explores war and its effect on human nature against the background of the natural world. It is also a strong love story that describes how a man and a woman, separated by war, struggle to keep their feelings for each other alive.

Born in 1950, Charles Frazier taught English literature at American universities and wrote short stories and travel books before writing *Cold Mountain*, his first novel, at the age of 46. The idea for the story came from the real-life journey of Frazier's great-great-uncle, W.P. Inman, back to his mountain home during the Civil War. The novel was an immediate success, winning a national book prize. A movie of the novel, starring Nicole Kidman and Jude Law, came out in 2003.

Chapter 1   The View from the Window

At the first light of dawn, flies began gathering around Inman's eyes and the long wound in his neck. Their touch woke him immediately. He brushed them away and looked across to the big window that faced his bed. During the day, he could see to the red road and the low brick wall. And beyond them to the fields and woods that stretched away to the west. But it was too early still for such a view, and only a gray light showed.

Inman rose and dressed and sat in a straight-backed chair, putting the shadowy room of beds and broken men behind him. Once again he looked through the window. It was as tall as a door, and he had imagined many times that it would open onto some other place and let him walk through and be there. During his first weeks in the hospital, when he had hardly been able to move his head, he had at least been able to watch out the window and picture the old green places he remembered from home. Childhood places. The corner of a field where long grasses grew. The branch of a tree on which he had often sat, watching his father drive cows home in the evening.

By now he had stared at the window all through a late summer so hot and wet that tiny black mushrooms grew overnight from the pages of his book. Inman suspected that the gray window had finally said all it had to say. This morning, though, it surprised him, because it brought him a lost memory of sitting in school beside a similar tall window, looking out over fields and low green hills to the great height of Cold Mountain.

It was September. The teacher was a round little man, hairless and pink-faced. He talked through the morning about history, teaching the older students about grand wars fought in ancient England. After ignoring him for a time, the young Inman had taken his hat from under his desk and thrown it through the window. It flew high in the air and landed at the edge of a field. The teacher saw what Inman had done and told him to get it and to come back and be beaten. Inman never knew why he did what he did, but he stepped out the door, put the hat on his head, and walked away. He never returned.

The memory passed as the day grew lighter. Inman thought, as he often did, of how he had received his wound during fighting outside Petersburg, in the state of Virginia. When his two closest friends had pulled away his clothes and looked at his neck, they had said a sad goodbye. "We'll meet again in a better world," they said. The doctors at the local hospital had also expected him to die. After two days they had sent him on to a hospital in North Carolina, his own state. There, the doctors looked at him and said that there was not much they could do. He might live or he might not. But slowly, the wound had started to heal.

Inman thought of the battles he had fought in, in this terrible civil war—Malvern Hill, Sharpsburg, Petersburg. Fredericksburg was another battle he would never forget. He thought back to how the fog had lifted that morning to show a great army marching uphill toward a stone wall. Inman had joined the men who were already behind the wall. They were well-protected there, as you could stand up comfortably and still be in the shelter of the wall, while the Federals* had to come uphill across open ground. It was a cold day, and the mud of the road was nearly frozen. The men let the Federals come very near before shooting them down. From behind the wall, Inman could hear the sound of bullets hitting meat. Thousands of Federals marched toward the wall all through the day, climbing the hill to be shot down. Inman started hating them for their stupid desire to die.

Late in the afternoon, the Federals had stopped attacking and

*Federals ("Feds"): soldiers from the northern states

2

the shooting slowly stopped. Thousands of men lay dead and dying on the hillside below the wall. The men on Inman's side who had no boots had climbed over the wall to pull the boots off the dead. That night Inman, too, went out onto the battlefield. The Federals lay on the ground in bloody piles, body parts everywhere. Inman's only thought, looking on the enemy, was, "Go home." He saw a man killing a group of badly wounded Federals by striking them on the head with a hammer. The man did it without anger, just moving from one to another, whistling softly.

Now, in the hospital, Inman often dreamed that the bloody pieces—arms, heads, legs—slowly came together and formed bodies whose parts did not match. They waved bloody arms, speaking the names of their women or singing lines of a song again and again. One figure, whose wounds were so terrible that he looked more like a piece of meat than a man, tried to rise but could not. He lay still but turned his head to stare at Inman with dead eyes, and spoke Inman's name in a low voice. Every morning after that dream, Inman woke in the blackest of moods.

♦

Some days later, Inman walked from the hospital into town. His neck hurt very badly but his legs felt strong, and that worried him. As soon as he was strong enough to fight, they would send him back to Virginia. He decided that he must be careful not to look too fit in front of a doctor.

Money had come from home and he had also received his pay from the army, so he walked through the streets and bought various things that he needed—a black woolen suit that fitted him perfectly, a black hat, strong boots, two knives, a little pot and cup, bullets for his pistol. Tired, he stopped at a coffee house and slowly drank a cup of something that was supposed to be coffee. He sat with his back straight, looking stiff and uncomfortable in his black suit, with the white bandage on his neck.

Inman picked up the newspaper he had bought, hoping to find something to interest him. On the third page he found a notice from the state government stating that deserters would be hunted down by an organization called the Home Guard. In another part of the paper he read that the Cherokee Indians* had been fighting the Federals. Inman put the paper down and wondered if his Cherokee friend, Swimmer, was among the men who were fighting. He had met Swimmer the summer they were both sixteen. Inman had been given the job of looking after some cows on Balsam Mountain. He had joined a group of men camping there, and after a few days a band of Cherokee Indians had camped a short distance away.

The Indians spent a lot of time playing a fast and dangerous ball game, and Swimmer had come over and invited the white men to play. The two groups had camped side by side for two weeks, the younger men playing the ball game most of the day. They spent the night drinking and telling stories by the fireside, eating great piles of freshly caught fish.

There in the highlands, the weather was almost always clear, and the view stretched across rows of blue mountains. Once, Swimmer had looked out over the mountains and said he believed Cold Mountain to be the chief mountain of the world. Inman asked how he knew that to be true, and Swimmer had simply replied, "Do you see a bigger one?"

In the mornings, when fog lay low in the valleys, Inman used to walk down to a cove to fish with Swimmer for an hour or two. There, Swimmer talked in a low voice, telling stories of animals and how they became as they are. He told of ways to cause sickness or death, how to protect a traveler on the road at night, and how to make the road seem short. Swimmer saw man's spirit as a weak thing, constantly under attack, always threatening to die inside you.

* Cherokee Indians: a North American native people

4

After many days, the weather turned wet and the two camps separated. Thinking of Swimmer now, Inman hoped that his friend was not out fighting Federals but living in a hut by a rushing stream.

He raised his coffee cup to his lips and found it cold and nearly empty. Inman guessed that Swimmer was right to say that a man's spirit could die while his body continued living. Inman felt that his spirit had been burned out of him, but he was still walking. He felt as dead as a tree that had been hit by lightning.

As Inman sat thinking of his loss, one of Swimmer's stories rushed into his memory. Swimmer claimed that above the blue sky there was a forest where a heavenly race lived. Men could not go there to stay and live, but in that high land a dead spirit could be reborn. Swimmer said that the tops of the highest mountains reached into this healing place. Now, as he sat in the coffee house, Cold Mountain came to Inman's mind as a place where his spirit might be healed. He could not bear the idea that this world was all that there was. So he held to the idea of another world, a better world, and he thought that Cold Mountain was probably a good place for it.

Inman took off his new coat and started working on a letter. It was long, and as the afternoon passed he drank several more cups of coffee. This was part of what he wrote:

I am coming home and I do not know how things are between us. Do you remember that night before Christmas four years ago when you told me that you would like to sit there forever and rest your head on my shoulder? Now I am sure that if you knew what I have seen and done, it would make you fear to do the same again.

Inman stood up and folded the letter. He put his hand up to the wound in his neck. The doctors claimed he was healing quickly, but it still hurt to talk and to eat, and sometimes to breathe. But on the walk down the street to mail the letter and then back out to the hospital, his legs felt surprisingly strong and willing.

After supper, Inman checked the knapsack under his bed. There was a blanket already in the bag and to these he added the cup and little pot and the knives. The knapsack had for some time been filled with hardtack, salt pork, a little dried beef, and some cornmeal.

He got in bed and pulled up the covers. Tired from his day of walking about town, Inman read only for a short time before falling asleep. He woke sometime deep in the night. The room was black and the only sounds were of men breathing and moving about in their beds. He rose and dressed in his new clothes. Then he put on his knapsack and went to the tall open window and looked out. Fog moved low on the ground, though the sky was clear. He stepped out of the window.

Chapter 2   Ada Monroe

Ada sat in the porch of the house that was now hers, writing a letter. Putting the point of the pen in ink, she wrote:

This you must know: although you have been away for so long, I will never hide a single thought from you. I believe it is our duty to be honest with each other and unlock our hearts.

She blew the paper to dry it and then carefully read her letter. She decided that she did not like what she had written and threw the letter away. Aloud she said, "That is just the way people talk. It means nothing."

She looked over to the kitchen garden, where tomatoes and beans grew that were hardly bigger than her thumb, although it was the growing season. Many of the leaves were eaten away by insects. Beyond the failed garden lay the old cornfield, now grown wild. Above the fields, the mountains showed faintly through the morning fog.

Ada sat waiting for the mountains to show themselves clearly.

The house and gardens were now in a terrible condition and Ada felt comforted that at least the mountains were as they should be. Since her father's funeral, Ada had done hardly any work on the farm. She had at least milked Waldo, the cow, and fed Ralph, the horse, but she had not done much more because she did not know how to do much more. She had left the chickens to look after themselves and they had grown thin and wild, and it had become more and more difficult to find their eggs.

Cookery was now a real problem for Ada. She was constantly hungry, having eaten little through the summer except milk, fried eggs, salads, and tiny tomatoes. She had been unable to make butter. She wanted to eat a chicken dish followed by a cake, but had no idea how to prepare such a meal.

Ada rose and started looking for eggs. She searched everywhere but found nothing. Remembering that a red hen sometimes sat in the big bushes on either side of the front steps, she went to one of the bushes and tried to look inside it. Folding her skirt tightly around her, she went on her hands and knees into the empty space in the center of the bush. There were no eggs there, but as she sat there she was reminded of times in her childhood when she and her cousin Lucy had hidden in bushes like this one. Looking up through the leaves at the pale sky, Ada realized that she wished never to leave this fine shelter. When she thought about what had happened to her recently, she wondered how her father had allowed her to grow up so impractical.

She had grown up in Charleston, and her father had given her an education far better than most young girls received. She had become a clever, loving daughter, filled with opinions on art and politics and literature. She could speak French and Latin quite well, and spoke a little Greek. She was able to sew and play the piano and was talented at painting and drawing. She read a lot. But none of these things helped her now, as the owner of a medium-sized farm, and she had no idea how to look after it.

All her life, Ada's father had kept her away from hard work. He had hired workers to help on the farm, and a man and his part-Cherokee Indian wife to help in the house, so that Ada only had to plan the weekly menus. She had therefore been free to spend her time reading, sewing, drawing, and practicing her music. But now the hired people were gone, leaving Ada to manage on her own.

Suddenly, the red hen came flying through the leaves, followed by the big black and gold rooster. He looked at her with his shining black eyes for a moment, then flew at her face. Ada threw up a hand to protect herself and was cut across the wrist. She knocked the bird to the ground but he flew at her again, and she escaped from the bush with the rooster scratching at her legs. She hit the bird until it fell away, and ran into the house, where she sank into an armchair and examined her wounds. There was blood on her wrist and scratches on her leg, and her skirt was torn. This is the place I have reached, she thought. I am living in a world where this is your reward for looking for eggs.

She rose and climbed the stairs to her room, removed her clothes, and washed. Finding no clean clothes, she took some from near the bottom of the dirty clothes pile. She wondered how to get through the hours until bedtime. Since the death of her father, Monroe, she had sorted out his things, his clothes and papers, but that was all she had done. Now, at the end of each empty day, the answer to the question, "What have you achieved today?" was always, "Nothing."

Ada took a book from her bedside table and went to sit in the upper hall in her father's old armchair by the window, where the light was good. She had spent much of the past three months sitting in the armchair reading. She liked the fact that when she looked up from the page, she could see the fields and mountains, and the great height of Cold Mountain above them all. It had been a wet summer and the mountains, with their fogs, clouds, and gray rain, were very different from her home town of Charleston.

She began to read, but could not stop thinking about food. She had not yet eaten breakfast, although it would soon be time for lunch. She went down to the kitchen and spent nearly two hours trying to make a loaf of bread. But when the loaf came out of the oven, it looked like badly made hardtack. Ada tried a piece, then threw it outside for the chickens. For lunch she ate only a plate of the little tomatoes and two apples.

Leaving her dirty plate and fork on the table, Ada went to the porch and stood looking. The sky was cloudless. She walked down the path a little way and turned onto the river road, picking wild flowers as she went. In fifteen minutes she reached the little church that had been Monroe's responsibility. Ada climbed the hill and went behind the church and stood beside Monroe's grave. She put the flowers on the ground and picked up the previous bunch, now wet and dying.

The day Monroe had died was in May. Late that afternoon, Ada had prepared to go out for a time to paint the flowers by the stream. As she left the house, she stopped to speak to Monroe, who sat reading a book under the apple tree in the yard. He seemed tired and said he would sleep, and asked her to wake him when she returned.

Ada was away for less than an hour. As she walked from the fields into the yard, she saw that he was lying with his mouth open. She walked up to wake him, but as she approached she could see that his eyes were open, his book fallen into the grass. She ran the last three steps and put her hand to his shoulder to shake him, but she knew immediately that he was dead.

Ada went as fast as she could for help, running and walking to her nearest neighbors, the Swangers. They were members of her father's church, and Ada had known them from her earliest days in the mountains. She reached their house breathless and crying. It had started raining, and when she and Esco Swanger got back to the cove, Monroe's body was wet and leaves had fallen on his face.

She had spent the night in the Swangers' house, lying awake and dry-eyed, longing for her dead father.

Two days later, she had buried Monroe on the little hill above the Pigeon River. The morning was bright and windy. Forty people, dressed in black, nearly filled the little church. Three or four men talked of Monroe's fine qualities, his small acts of kindness, and his wise advice. Esco Swanger spoke of Ada and her terrible loss, of how she would be missed when she returned to her home in Charleston.

Then, later, they had all stood and watched the burial. Afterward, Sally Swanger had taken Ada by the elbow and walked with her down the hill.

"You stay with us until you can arrange to go back to Charleston," she said.

Ada stopped and looked at her. "I will not be returning to Charleston immediately," she said. "I will be staying at Black Cove, at least for a time."

Mrs. Swanger stared at her. "How will you manage?" she asked.

"I'm not sure," Ada said.

"You're not going up to that big dark house by yourself today. Take dinner with us and stay until you're ready to leave."

"I would be grateful," said Ada.

She had stayed with the Swangers for three days and then returned to the empty house, frightened and alone. It was a brave decision, as the war was not going well for the southern states. The Federals were just over the mountains to the north, and according to the newspapers, things were growing desperate in Virginia. People worried that the Federals would soon come south looking for food, take what they wanted, and leave people with nothing. Everyone in town knew how the Feds had robbed a family, taking every animal and piece of food they could find, and setting fire to the henhouse as they left.

The Home Guard was as bad or worse. The story was that

Teague and his men had thrown a family called the Owens out into their yard at dinnertime. Teague claimed they were known to be lovers of the Federals. First they searched the house, and then they examined the yard to see if they could find soft dirt from fresh digging. They hit the man and later hit his wife. Then they hanged a pair of dogs, tied the woman's thumbs together behind her back, and pulled her up by them with a rope thrown over a tree. But the man still wouldn't say where he had hidden the silver.

A white-headed boy called Birch had said he believed that maybe they should stop and leave. But Teague pointed a pistol at him and said, "I won't be told how to treat these people. I'll do exactly what I like." In the end, they didn't kill anybody and didn't find the silver either, but just lost interest and left.

◆

Walking back home from her father's grave, Ada stopped to rest by a rock that had a view of the river valley. She looked up toward Cold Mountain, pale and gray and distant, then down into Black Cove. She knew that if she stayed, she would need help, but she doubted that she could find anyone, since all the men fit to work were fighting in the war. She sat and looked down at the farm. It seemed a mystery to her that she owned the farm, though she could say exactly how it had happened.

She and her father had come to the mountains six years earlier, hoping to find a cure for the illness that was slowly destroying Monroe, so that he coughed up blood each day. His Charleston doctor had recommended living in the mountains, and Monroe had found a mountain church that needed a preacher.

They had set off immediately, traveling first by train to Spartanburg, where they had stayed for several days, and then by horse and carriage. They had left Spartanburg in the hour before dawn, and had traveled all through the day, through land that climbed higher and higher. As the day went on, Ada became certain that the road would disappear completely, leaving them lost in a wild country. Monroe, however, was excited and from time to time spoke poetry aloud. Ada had laughed and kissed him, thinking that she would follow him anywhere. It was long after midnight when they came to a dark little church on a hill above the road and a river. They went in out of the rain and lay down in their wet clothes. The next morning Monroe rose stiffly and walked outside. Ada heard him laugh and then say, "My God, I thank you once again." She went to him. He stood in front of the church, laughing and pointing above the door. She turned and read the sign: Cold Mountain Church.

"We have arrived home," Monroe said.

In the weeks that followed their arrival, Ada and Monroe had visited members of the church and others who they hoped would join it. People seemed distant and quite cold. Only the men would come out to meet them, and sometimes Monroe and Ada would be invited in and sometimes not. When they were invited inside, the men looked at the fire and did not speak. When Monroe asked a direct question, often they just looked at him. There were hidden people in the house—women, children, and old people—but they never introduced themselves. To Ada, these people seemed to care nothing at all for the things she and Monroe knew. These mountain people clearly saw life very differently.

But Monroe and Ada remained at the church, living in a little riverside house that belonged with it. Then, when Monroe's health improved and people seemed to be accepting him, Monroe sold the Charleston house and bought the cove from the Black family. He liked the way the land was flat and open at the bottom of the cove, and he liked the wooded hillsides that rose from the farm toward Cold Mountain, and the ice cold water from the stream. And he especially liked the house he had built there, with its big porch all across the front, and the great fireplace in the sitting room. When he bought the cove, the place had been a farm, but

Monroe did not bother to manage the farm well, since he had put his money into rice and cotton and did not need to grow his own food.

Still seated by the rock, Ada took a letter from her pocket and began to read it. It was from her father's lawyer in Charleston, and in it he informed her that due to the war, Ada's income from rice and cotton had been reduced to almost nothing. Ada stood up, put the letter back in her pocket, and took the path down to Black Cove. She wondered how she would find the courage to hope. When she reached the old stone wall that marked the edge of the farm, she paused again. It was a lovely spot, one of her favorite corners of the farm. The wall went north to south, and on this sunny afternoon it was warm with afternoon sun. An apple tree grew near it, and a few early apples had fallen into the tall grass. Ada thought it was the most peaceful place she had ever known. She settled herself against the wall, took her book from her pocket and began reading, until eventually she fell asleep in the long grass.

When she woke, it was dark, and a half-moon stood high in the sky. She had never spent a night in the woods alone, but she was less frightened than she expected. She sat for hours watching the progress of the moon across the sky, until the first gray light appeared. In her mind, she considered the possibilities again and again. They were few. If she tried to sell Black Cove and return to Charleston, the little money she would receive would not last long. After a time, she would have to live with friends of her father, probably as a teacher to their children.

It was that or marry. But the thought of returning to Charleston in order to hunt for a man disgusted her. She tried to see herself saying to someone that she loved him, when she actually meant that she needed his money. But she could not imagine the marriage act with such a man.

She knew that if she returned to Charleston under these conditions, she could not expect people to welcome her, because in the opinion of Charleston society she had refused too many men who had shown an interest in her. She had told too many of her friends that these men bored her and that marriage was not a woman's only purpose in life. As a result, many people thought that she was very strange. In the year before they had moved to the mountains, Ada had lost many friends. So even now, the idea of returning to Charleston was a bitter thought. There was nothing pulling her back and she had no family there.

And although she was an outsider, this place, the blue mountains, seemed to be holding her where she was. The only thought that left her any hope of happiness was this: the land that she could see around her was her own, belonged to her.

She returned to the house in the early morning, and was sitting in the porch some hours later, wondering what her next action should be, when she saw a figure come walking up the road. It was a girl, a short one, thin as a chicken neck except across the lower half of her body, where she was quite wide. The girl came up to the porch and, without asking permission, sat in the chair next to Ada. She wore a blue, square-necked dress made of cheap cloth.

"Sally Swanger said you're in need of help," she said.

Ada examined the girl carefully. She was a dark thing, with a thin chest but strong-looking arms. She had a broad nose and her hair was black and thick. Big dark eyes, no shoes, clean feet.

"Mrs. Swanger is right. I do need help," Ada said, "but I need help with the farm. It's rough work and I believe I need a man for the job."

"Number one," the girl said, "if you have a horse, I can plow all day. Number two, every man worth hiring has gone to fight."

The girl's name, Ada soon discovered, was Ruby, and after talking for a time, Ada began to think that Ruby was strong enough to work on the farm. Just as importantly, as they talked, Ada liked Ruby and felt that she had a willing heart. And though

14

Ruby could not read a word or even write her name, Ada thought she saw in her something hard and bright. And they shared this: Ruby was a motherless child from the day she was born. In a short time, and to Ada's surprise, they came to an agreement.

Ada said, "At the moment, and possibly for some months, I have very little money."

"Money isn't important," Ruby said. "Sally said you needed help, and she was right. But I don't want to be your servant. I'm saying, if I'm going to help you here, both of us must understand that."

As they talked, the black and gold rooster walked by the porch and paused to stare at them.

"I hate that bird," Ada said. "He attacked me."

Ruby said, "I wouldn't keep a bird that did that to me."

"But how can I get rid of it?" Ada said.

Ruby looked at her in surprise. She rose and quickly seized the rooster, put his body under her left arm, and with her right hand pulled off his head. He struggled for a minute and then went still. Ruby threw the head into a bush.

"He'll need cooking for quite a time," she said.

By dinnertime the meat of the rooster was falling from the bones, and bread was baking in the oven.

Chapter 3   The Journey Begins

It was dawn and the golden sunlight shone down on a tall man in a black hat, with a knapsack on his back, walking west. After the lonely, wet nights he had recently spent, Inman felt half-dead. He stopped and put his boot on the roadside fence, and looked out across the fields. He tried to greet the day with a thankful heart, but he hated this flat land, with its red dirt and bad smell. The wound in his neck felt freshly raw and hurt badly. He put a finger

15

underneath the bandage, and to his surprise realized that the wound had healed over and was no longer a deep red hole.

He calculated that although he had been walking for some days, he had not traveled a great distance from the hospital. His wound forced him to walk slowly and rest more often than he wished. He was very tired and also rather lost, still trying to find a route that went directly toward his home in the Appalachian mountains. But the country consisted of small farms, all cut up by tiny paths that crossed each other, with no signs to say where they were going. He kept feeling that he had been led further south than he wanted. And the weather had been bad, with rain that came suddenly, with thunder and lightning, day and night. Each farm had two or three dogs and he was often forced to fight off their attacks. The dogs and the danger of the Home Guard meant that he was always nervous traveling through the dark nights.

The previous night had been the worst. He had heard the sound of horses and had climbed a tree and watched as a pack of Home Guard came by, searching for men like him to seize and beat and return to the army. When he had climbed down and begun walking again, every tree seemed to have the shape of a man, and once he aimed his pistol at a bush that looked like a fat man with a big hat.

That long night finished, his greatest desire now was to climb over the fence, walk out across the fields into the woods, and sleep. But having at last reached open country, he needed to move on, so he took his foot off the fence and continued walking. The sun climbed the sky and turned hot, and all the insect world seemed interested in Inman's body. In the afternoon he came to a small village with a store and a few houses. Inman decided to risk going to the store to buy food. He put his pistol into his blanket roll in order to look harmless and not attract attention.

Two men sitting on the porch hardly looked up as he climbed the steps. One man was hatless, with his hair standing up on his head. The other man, who wore a cap, was studying a newspaper. Leaning against the wall behind him was an expensive gun. Inman wondered what men like these were doing with such a good gun. He walked past them into the store and they still did not look up. The store did not have much, but Inman bought cornmeal, a piece of cheese, some hardtack, and then he went out onto the porch. The two men were gone. Inman stepped down into the road to go on walking west, eating as he traveled. A pair of black dogs crossed the road in front of him.

Then, as Inman came to the edge of the town, the two men who had been on the porch suddenly came from behind a house and stood in front of him. They were not big men, they were drunk, maybe, and seemed too confident.

"Where are you going, you fool?" the man with the cap said.

Inman said nothing. He finished his food with two big bites. Before the war he had never much liked fighting, but when he had joined the army, he had discovered that fighting was easy for him. He had decided that it was like any other thing, a gift. The two men jumped on him before he even had time to remove his pack. But Inman fought them off and beat both of them to the ground, so that they lay quiet, face down. Then the hatless man rolled over and pulled out a small pistol. Inman seized the pistol and beat the man on the head with it, threw it onto the roof of a building, and walked away.

Outside the town, he turned into the woods and walked away from the road. All through the afternoon he continued west through the woods, stopping now and again to listen for anyone following. Sometimes he thought he heard voices in the distance, but they were faint and were probably his imagination. Night came, and as he walked, Inman's thoughts went back to his home in the mountains, and he remembered the day he first saw Ada.

◆

Inman had attended church especially to see Ada. In the weeks following her arrival in Cold Mountain, he had heard much about her before he saw her. She and her father had caused a lot of amusement among the houses along the river road. People sat on the porch, as at the theater, eager to watch Ada and Monroe pass by in their carriage. All agreed that Ada was pretty, but they laughed at her Charleston clothes and hairstyles. If they saw her holding a flower in order to admire its color, or bending to touch a leaf, some called her mad. People could not understand her habit of staring at a thing—bird, or bush, sunset, mountain—and then scratching at a piece of paper with her pen.

So one Sunday morning Inman dressed himself carefully—in a new black suit, white shirt, black tie, black hat—and went to church to take a look at Ada. It had rained and the road was muddy, so that he arrived late and had to take a seat at the back. He could only see the backs of people's heads, but he recognized Ada immediately, since her dark hair was twisted up on her head in a style that was not known in the mountains. A few fine curls lay on her soft neck, and all through the church service, Inman's eyes remained on her white skin. After a while, even before he saw her face, he wanted to press two fingers against the back of her neck.

That morning Monroe preached, as he often did, about the question that worried him most: Why was man born to die? He had no real answer, and people had become bored with his constant questioning. Inman sat staring at Ada's neck, not really listening to Monroe's words, waiting for him to finish.

When the service ended, the men and women left the church by separate doors. The men lined up to shake hands with Monroe and then they all chatted with each other and discussed whether it would rain again. Ada stood on the edge of the group, looking foreign and beautiful and very uncomfortable. Everyone else wore warm woolen clothes, but she was wearing a light, cream-colored dress that did not suit the weather at all. The older women came to her and said things, and then there were embarrassed pauses and they walked away.

"If I went and told her my name, do you think she'd answer me?" said a man who had come to church for exactly the same reason as Inman.

"I couldn't say," Inman replied.

"You haven't an idea how to begin talking to her," another man laughed.

Inman walked away from the group towards Sally Swanger. "I'll do some work on your farm if you'll introduce me," he said.

Sally laughed. "Notice I'm not even asking who to," she said.

"Now's the time," Inman replied.

Mrs. Swanger took Inman's black coat by the sleeve and pulled him across the yard to Ada. He raised his hand to take off his hat.

"Miss Monroe," Sally Swanger said, her face bright, "Mr. Inman has asked to meet you. You've met his parents. His people built the church."

Mrs. Swanger walked away and Ada looked Inman directly in the face. He realized too late that he had not planned what to say.

"Yes?" said Ada. There was not much patience in her voice, and for some reason Inman was amused. He held his hat and looked into it, hoping for an idea.

"You're free to put your hat back on, and say something," Ada said.

"You know, people are very interested in you," said Inman.

"A new experience, am I?" Ada asked.

"No," Inman said.

"Then what would you compare me to?"

"Like picking up a thistle," Inman said.

Ada smiled, liking the comparison. "Tell me this," she said. "A woman earlier said that it was sheep-killing weather. Did she mean it was good weather for killing sheep, or that this weather killed sheep?"

19

"The first," Inman said.

"Well, then, I thank you. You've been useful to me."

She turned and walked away to her father. Inman watched her touch Monroe's arm and say something to him, and they went to the carriage and drove off.

◆

Late in the night, Inman followed a rough road that ran along the banks of the Deep River. It soon went down into a gorge, with high rocks on either side, so that there was only a piece of sky above. It was so dark for a time that Inman had to feel with his feet for the soft dust of the road to find the way. He did not like his position and feared the Home Guard horsemen would find him before he could find a place to leave the road.

Although it was painful, he started to run, and some minutes later he saw a light ahead. As he approached, he saw that a man was standing in the road, holding a lamp. Walking quietly, Inman came closer and stopped by a rock less than ten meters away. The man wore a suit of black clothes and a white shirt. He held a horse by a rope tied around its neck. In the light Inman could see that the horse carried something white across its back.

"Lord, oh Lord!" the man cried. His whole body was shaking and he seemed desperate. Then he walked to the horse and lifted the white object off the animal, and Inman could see that he was carrying a woman, with her black hair brushing the ground. Inman realized that the man was taking her to the edge of the gorge. He could hear the man crying in the dark as he walked.

Inman took out his pistol and ran along the road toward the man. "Put her down," he said.

She dropped at the man's feet.

"What pistol is that?" the man said.

"Step away from her," Inman said. "Get over there where I can see you."

The man stepped across the body and approached Inman. "You're a message from God saying no," the man said. He fell to his knees in the road and Inman saw that his face was shiny with tears. Inman hit him lightly with the pistol so that he fell in the road on his back.

"You deserve to be killed," Inman said.

"Don't kill me, I'm a preacher," the man replied.

Inman showed his surprise.

"Is she dead?" he asked.

"No. She has a child inside her. And I gave her some powder to make her sleep for four hours."

"Not married to her?"

"No."

Inman stepped over to the girl, put a hand to her dark head, and lifted it. She looked drugged, but he could see that she might be attractive.

"Put her back on the horse," Inman said.

The man did as he was told, and then said, "What now?"

"Where did you come from?" Inman asked.

"There's a town not far off," the man replied, pointing up the road in the direction Inman was going.

"Walk in front of me and show me the way," Inman said.

They started walking. Inman kept his pistol in one hand and led the horse with the other. The road soon started climbing through low hills. They walked in silence for some time, until finally the preacher said, "What do you intend doing with me?"

"I'm thinking about it," Inman said. "How did you get into this trouble?"

"It's hard to say. No one in town knows about us. She lives with her deaf old grandmother, and it was easy for her to come away at midnight and lie on a river bank with me until the first birds began to sing."

"You were going to throw her into the gorge like a dead pig."

"Well, yes, but I had to think about my position. If we had been found out, I would have been chased out of town. Believe me, I spent many nights worrying about what to do."

"Why didn't you marry her?"

"I had already asked another woman to marry me."

"Then you shouldn't be a preacher," Inman said.

They walked on and came to a small town on the river bank.

"I'll tell you what we're going to do," Inman said. "We're going to put her back in her bed."

They entered the town. "Which house?" Inman said.

The preacher pointed down the road to a tiny house. When they reached it, Inman took the rope off the horse and tied the preacher by his neck to a tree.

"Stand here quietly and we'll live through this," he said.

He lifted the girl from the horse, with one arm under her waist and another under her soft legs. Her dark head rested helplessly on his shoulder. "I ought to kill him," Inman thought. He carried the girl to the house, put her down by a bush, and looked in through a window. An old lady slept on a bed by the fire, with her mouth open. The door was not locked and Inman put his head inside. "Hey," he said, but the old lady did not move. There was an empty bed at the end of the room, and Inman stepped outside, picked the girl up, and carried her to the bed. He pulled off her shoes and covered her to her chin. Then he left her and walked back out to where the preacher stood tied to the tree. He took pen and ink and paper from his knapsack, and found a place where the moonlight came through the trees. He wrote the story down, then put the paper in a tree branch where the preacher could not reach it.

The preacher watched him and when he guessed what Inman was writing, he kicked at him with his feet.

"You've ruined my life," he said.

"Don't blame that on me," Inman said. "I don't want to have to

22

wonder if you'll be back in that black gorge in a night or two with her lying on your horse again."

"Then shoot me and leave me."

"Don't think that I don't want to do that," Inman said as he walked away.

Chapter 4   Ruby

That first morning, Ada and Ruby agreed that Ruby would move to the cove and teach Ada how to manage a farm. There would be very little money involved in her pay. They would take most of their meals together, but Ruby did not want to live with anyone else and decided she would move into the old cabin near the house. After they had eaten their first dinner, Ruby went home and gathered her belongings. She came back to Black Cove with them, and seldom thought about the past again.

The two women spent their first days together listing the things that needed doing. They walked together around the farm, Ruby looking around a lot, talking constantly. She had ideas about everything. The most urgent matter, she said, was to start a good vegetable garden. She suggested that they clear the old cornfield. She wanted more chickens and thought of buying a pig. She was delighted by the number of apple trees, and said that they could sell the apples in October. She was also pleased with the tobacco field. The tobacco plants were tall and strong, and she thought they could sell them in exchange for seed and salt and other things they could not produce themselves.

When Ada told Ruby how little money she had, Ruby said, "I've never held a piece of money bigger than a dollar in my hand." Ruby's opinion was that they did not really need cash. Ruby had never felt comfortable with money, especially when she thought of how one could hunt, gather, and plant the things one needed. And it was true that now, with the war, money had lost so much value that it was hard to buy anything with it anyway. On their first trip together into town, they could not believe that they had paid five dollars for a small packet of needles. And the cloth that they wanted was priced at fifty dollars. Ruby said that if they had sheep they could make the cloth themselves. Ada could only think that it would take many days of hard work. Money made things so much easier.

But even if they had it, store owners really didn't want money, since the value of it was likely to fall almost immediately. The general feeling was that paper money ought to be spent as soon as possible. It was wiser to exchange food and other goods. Ruby seemed to understand this.

Ruby's plan was this: Ada should sell either the carriage or the piano. She believed she could exchange either one or the other for the things they would need to get through the winter. Ada thought about this for two days, and finally surprised herself by deciding to sell the piano. She did not play the piano particularly well, and it had been Monroe who had wanted her to learn. Also, she knew that she would have very little time for art in her future life and that she would spend most of the free time she had drawing and painting.

After Ada had taken her decision, Ruby wasted no time. She knew who had extra animals and food, and she decided on Old Jones who lived up on East Fork, and whose wife had wanted the piano for some time. Ruby was a hard bargainer, and Jones was finally made to give a fine pig, half a dozen sheep, and large quantities of cornmeal, green vegetables, and smoked meat.

In a few days, Ruby brought the pigs and the little sheep up into Black Cove. She took them to Cold Mountain to feed through the fall, and marked their ears with a knife to show who their owner was. Late one afternoon, Old Jones arrived with another man and took the piano away. Ada sat on the porch and watched it go. She did not feel much regret, but she thought about the party that Monroe had given four days before Christmas in the last winter before the war.

♦

The chairs in the room had been pushed back against the wall to make space for dancing, and people who could play the piano each played for a short time. There were pretty lamps in glass bowls, a fashion that no one in the mountains had seen before. On the dining room table there were tiny cookies, cakes and brown bread, and sweet-smelling pots of tea.

In the early evening, people sat and talked in groups of the same sex. Ada sat with the women but looked interestedly around the room. Six old men sat in chairs near the fire and discussed the worsening political situation. The sons of the most valued members of the church sat in a corner of the room and talked loudly. Women of mixed ages sat in another corner. Sally Swanger wore a new pair of fine shoes, and sat waiting for comments on them, holding her legs stiffly out in front of her. Later the groups mixed, and some stood around the piano and sang, and then some of the younger people danced.

As the evening continued, Ada realized that she had had too much to drink. Her face felt hot and her neck was wet under her pretty green dress. Sally Swanger, who had also had too many glasses of wine, took Ada's arm and in a whisper said, "That Inman boy's just got here. I shouldn't say this, but you ought to marry him. The two of you'd make pretty brown-eyed babies."

Ada had been shocked by the comment, and her face had gone bright red, so that she had to go to the kitchen to calm herself. But there she was surprised to find Inman alone, sitting in the stove corner. He had arrived late, having ridden through a slow winter rain, and he was warming up and drying out before joining the party. He wore a black suit and sat with his legs crossed.

"Oh," Ada said. "There you are. The ladies are already so pleased to know you're here."

"The old ladies?" Inman said.

"Well, everyone. Mrs. Swanger is especially pleased by your arrival."

This comment reminded Ada of Mrs. Swanger's words to her, and the blood rushed to her head.

"Are you all right?" Inman asked.

"Yes, but it's hot in here."

Ada went to the door and opened it for a breath of cool air. Out from the dark, over a great distance, came the high lonely call of a wild dog.

"That's a sad sound," Inman said.

Ada closed the door and turned to Inman, but when she did the heat of the room, and the alcohol, and the soft look on Inman's face, made her feel faint. She took a few uncertain steps and when Inman half stood and put out a hand to steady her, she took it. And then, she didn't know how, she found herself in his lap. He put his hands on her shoulders for a moment, and she lay back with her head beneath his chin. Ada remembered thinking that she never wanted to leave this place, but did not realize that she had said it aloud. He seemed as content as she was and he moved his hands to her shoulders and held her there.

She rested in his lap for half a minute, no more. Then she was up and away, and she remembered turning at the door to look back at him, where he sat with a puzzled smile on his face.

Ada went back to the piano, where she played for quite some time. Inman eventually came and stood leaning against the door, watching her for a while before moving away to talk to a friend. Through the rest of the evening, neither Ada nor Inman mentioned what had taken place in the kitchen. They talked once, rather uncomfortably, and Inman left early.

◆

Ada sat on the porch for some minutes after the piano had gone. Then she and Ruby made and drank some real coffee. That morning Ada had discovered a large sack of green coffee beans in a dark corner of the barn. Over the next few days, they exchanged most of the coffee for sacks of salt, corn, potatoes and beans, and eight chickens. In these matters, Ruby was a ball of energy and she soon created a daily routine for herself and Ada. Each day before dawn she milked the cow, lit the fire in the kitchen, and made breakfast. Ada, who rarely got up before ten, started getting up at dawn too, since Ruby obviously expected her to do so. The two young women ate breakfast together, while Ruby talked about her plans for the day.

After breakfast was done, they worked constantly. On days when there was not one big thing to do, they did many small ones. That first month, Ruby made Ada understand that she needed to get her hands dirty if she wanted food on the table. She made Ada work when she did not want to, made her wear dirty clothes while she dug in the earth. She taught Ada how to turn cream into butter and how to cut the head off a chicken. And Ada did these things, because somewhere inside her, she knew that another person might walk away and let her fail. Ruby would not let her fail.

The only moments of rest were after the supper dishes had been put away. Then Ada and Ruby sat on the porch and Ada read aloud. Then, when it became too dark to read, Ada closed the book and asked Ruby about herself. Over a period of weeks, she learned the story of Ruby's life.

◆

Ruby had never known her mother, and her father, a man called Stobrod Thewes, had never had a job for more than a week or two. They lived in a cabin that had a dirt floor and no ceiling. On many mornings, Ruby had found snow on top of her bed cover when she woke. Stobrod did not look after their home, and in Ruby's opinion was little more than an animal.

Ruby had to find her own food soon after she learned to walk, and was forced to depend on the kindness of the women on neighboring farms. One night, when Ruby was four, she was returning from a farm when her dress got caught in a bush. Ruby spent the night by the bush, unable to get away. She never forgot those dark hours. It was cold near the river, and she remembered shaking with cold and crying for many hours, calling out for help, frightened of the wild animals that might come and eat her. But later she was spoken to by a voice in the dark. She felt that a gentle spirit had come to look after her. She remembered every star pattern that passed across the sky and every word spoken directly to her heart by the calm voice that comforted and protected her all through the night.

The next morning, a man found her and she walked home and never spoke a word to Stobrod about it. He did not ask where she had been. But she still heard the voice in her head, and after that night she seemed to know things that others had no idea about.

As she got older, she and Stobrod had lived off what Ruby grew on their little bit of land. Her father, who loved to drink, often disappeared for many days, walking fifty kilometers for a party, or going off into the woods. So everyone was surprised when, in the first days of the war, Stobrod joined the army. He rode off one morning, and Ruby had not heard from him since. As he had taken the horse, Ruby could not even plow the land. The first year of the war had been hard for her, but she had fed herself by using Stobrod's gun to go hunting in the woods.

At present, Ruby believed she was twenty-one years old, although Stobrod was not certain of either the year of her birth or the day. He could not even remember what season it had been when she arrived.

Chapter 5   The Home Guard

Inman walked through days of cooling weather, blue skies, and empty roads. He avoided towns and met few people, and the few he met were mainly slaves. The nights were warm and lit by big moons, and day after day passed with nothing much happening. As he walked, Inman often thought of Ada, and of one evening in particular, that Christmas four years ago when she had fallen into his lap.

It seemed like another life, another world. He remembered her weight on his legs, her softness, and the sweet smell of her hair. She had leaned back and rested her head on his shoulder. Then she had sat up and he had put his hands on her shoulders. He had wanted to put his arms around her and hold her tight, but she had stood up and pulled at her skirt, and smoothed her hair.

"Well," she had said. "Well."

Inman had leaned forward, and taken her hand and put his lips to her wrist. Ada had slowly taken her hand away and then stood looking down at it.

"That was unexpected," she said. Then she had walked away.

He was thinking of her once more when, one day in the early afternoon, he saw a figure in the distance behind him, walking fast. Inman waited until he came to a bend in the road, then he went into the woods and hid behind a tree trunk.

Soon, the walker came around the bend. He had no hair, and wore a long gray coat and carried a knapsack. As the man came nearer, it became plain that he had been badly beaten. When the man raised his blue eyes from the ground, Inman realized that it was the preacher.

Inman stepped into the road and said, "Hello."

The preacher stopped and stared. "Good God," he said.

"What happened to you?" said Inman.

"When they found me and read your note, a number of men

gave me a beating. They threw my clothes in the river and shaved my head. I was told to get out of town or they would hang me."

"I can imagine," Inman said. "What happened to the girl?"

"Oh, Laura Foster. She couldn't remember anything. When they discover she's going to have a child, people will talk about her for a time. In two or three years she'll marry an old man who wants a pretty woman."

Inman started walking along the road and the preacher, whose name was Veasey, started walking with him.

"Since you appear to be going west, I'll just walk with you, if you don't mind," he said.

"But I do mind," Inman said, thinking it was better to go alone than with a fool for a friend. But Veasey continued to walk beside him, talking all the time. He seemed desperate to tell Inman the story of his life and share all the mistakes he had made. He was not a success as a preacher—that was clear even to Veasey.

"I'm going to Texas to start a new life," Veasey said. "They say it's a land of freedom. I'll claim some land and keep cattle."

"And how will you buy your first cow?" Inman asked.

"With this." Veasey pulled a gun from under his coat. "I stole it a day or two ago."

He sounded as pleased as a boy who had stolen a cake from a neighbor's kitchen.

Inman and Veasey had not traveled far when they came to a tree that had been cut down. Beside it lay a long saw.

"Look," Veasey said. "Someone would pay a lot of money for that."

He went to pick it up and Inman said, "The woodcutters have just gone to get their dinners. They'll be back soon."

"I don't know about that. I just found a saw by the road. I'll sell it to the first man we meet," Veasey replied.

"For a preacher, you seem very happy to take other people's property," Inman said.

They walked on and after a time saw a man standing below the road, looking at a large black bull that lay dead in the shallow water of a stream. The man saw them passing and shouted to them for help. Inman climbed down, and Veasey put the saw by the roadside and followed.

They stood beside the man and looked at the bull, which had flies all around it. The man was in late middle age, with a big chest, dark eyes, and a little round mouth.

"How do you aim to get it out?" Veasey asked.

The man pointed to a rope that lay beside him. Inman looked at him and Veasey, then at the bull.

"We could try to pull it," he said. "But it's a big animal. We'd do better to think of another way."

The man ignored him and tied the rope onto the bull's neck and they all took hold of the rope and pulled. The body did not move. After some more useless pulling, without saying anything, Inman put down the rope and went back up to the road. He picked up the saw and returned to the bull, putting the saw to its neck.

"Somebody take the other end of this thing," he said.

Soon they had cut the animal up into sections, which they pulled out of the stream and left on the ground. The water was red with the animal's blood.

"I wouldn't drink that water for a few days," Inman said.

"Come and eat supper with us," the man said. "You can sleep in the barn."

"Only if you'll take that saw," Inman replied.

"I expect good money for it," Veasey said quickly.

"Take it for nothing," said Inman.

The man picked up the saw and the three men walked down the road, which followed the stream. They had not walked far when the man stopped and went to a big tree with a hole in its trunk. He put his arm into the hole and pulled out a bottle.

"I've a number of these hidden around for the right moment," he said.

They sat against the trunk of the tree and passed the bottle around. The man said his name was Junior, and he started telling stories about his youth and the number of women he had had. He said that all his troubles had begun when he had taken a wife, because three years after the wedding she had had a black baby. She had refused to name the father, and Junior had tried to separate from her, but the judge had not allowed it. She had later brought her two sisters to live with him and they had had children while unmarried.

Having told his stories, Junior led the two men to his house, which was only a short distance away. It was large and in such terrible condition that it stood at an angle to the ground. They walked into the main room, and Junior immediately went to a cupboard and took out a bottle and three cups. The floor, like the rest of the house, was at an angle, and when Inman sat down, he had to stop the chair from sliding over to the wall.

They drank for a time, and Inman became a little drunk. Soon, Veasey fell asleep where he sat. Then a young woman came wandering around the corner of the house and sat between Inman and Junior. She was fair-haired and round, and wore a cotton dress so thin and pale you could almost see her skin beneath it. Her hair was uncombed, and her dress was pulled up over her knees so that Inman could see the upper half of her legs.

Junior said to Inman, "Get this cow to feed you."

He rose and walked away. Inman followed the woman, who was called Lila, to the back of the house. There was a barn and a henhouse, and in the middle of the yard there was a big fire. Two more pale females appeared, obviously the sisters of Lila. They were followed by two dark-haired boys and a thin, pretty girl of eight or ten. They all gathered about the fire and Lila said, "Supper done?"

32

Nobody said anything, and one of the sisters picked up a pot and took a deep drink. She passed it along, and when it got to Inman he drank from it, and it was like nothing he had drunk before. The pot went around a number of times.

The sisters took some loaves from the fire and gave them to the children, who tore up the bread and put large pieces into their mouths before disappearing into the house. Then Lila came and stood next to Inman. She put a hand on his shoulder and said, "You're a big man."

Inman could not think what to reply. Then one of the other sisters came over and said, "Come eat." Inman carried his knapsack to the porch, and Lila reached out and put it down. As she turned to walk into the house, Inman took the knapsack and pushed it deep into a space between some wood piled high on the porch. He followed the women into the main room and saw that Veasey was still asleep. A lamp was smoking on the table, throwing shadows across the walls and floor. Lila sat Inman at the table, and one of the sisters brought a plate of meat in. Inman could not say what creature it came from. All three girls gathered around the table to watch him eat. Then Lila came over to him and rubbed her stomach against his shoulder.

"You're a fine-looking thing," she said.

Inman's arms and legs felt strangely heavy and he was unable to think clearly. The young woman took his left hand and put it up under her skirt.

"Get out," she said to the sisters, and they left.

She climbed onto the table and sat so that her legs were over him. Then she pulled the top of her dress down and leaned forward. At that moment the door opened and Junior appeared, holding a lamp in one hand and a gun in the other.

"What the hell's going on?" he said.

Inman sat back in his chair and watched as Junior pointed the gun at him. "This would be a terrible place to die," he thought, but he felt unable to move. Junior looked over to where Veasey slept. "Go wake him up," he said to Lila, and she went to Veasey and bent over him. He woke with her chest in his face, and smiled. Until he saw the gun.

"Now you get the other ones," Junior said to Lila. He walked over to her and hit her hard across the face. "Get up," he said to Inman.

Pointing a gun at the two men, Junior made them walk out onto the porch. Inman moved slowly and with an effort. Up at the road he could see faint movements in the dark. As they came nearer, he saw a band of Home Guards and, behind them, another group of men who were chained to each other.

"You're not the first one I've trapped here," Junior told Inman. "I get five dollars for every deserter I catch."

They tied Inman and Veasey to the string of prisoners and pushed them all against the wall of the house. None of the tied men said a word, but moved to the wall like half-dead creatures. They leaned back and immediately fell into open-mouthed sleep. But Inman and Veasey stayed awake, from time to time pulling uselessly at their ropes.

The Guards built up the fire in the yard until it stood as high as the walls of the house. After a time, one of them brought out a fiddle and started playing, while the other Guards drank from various pots. Then they danced around the fire and sometimes they could be seen pressing themselves against Lila or one of her sisters. When the men finally stopped dancing, Lila pushed herself against Inman. She looked him in the eye and said, "Bye bye." Then the Guards pointed their guns at the chained men and marched them off down the road toward the east.

♦

For several days, Inman walked tied by the wrists at the end of a long rope with fifteen other men. Veasey was tied directly in front

34

of Inman, and he walked with his head down, unable to believe his bad luck. Some of the chained men were old, others only boys, all of them accused of being deserters or of being on the side of the Federals. Inman understood that they were either being taken to prison or being returned to the fighting. As they walked, some men shouted that they were innocent, and others cried and begged to be freed.

The prisoners walked for several days, hardly speaking to each other at all. For food they were given nothing, and for drink they simply bent over a stream and used their hands to hold the water. The old men grew especially tired, and when they could no longer walk, even when pushed by a gun, they were given a mixture of milk and corn. Some days the Guards made the prisoners walk all day and they slept at night. Some days they slept and rose at sunset and started walking and continued all night. It did not make much difference, because the woods were so thick that the sun never seemed to shine through them. Inman felt weak and faint. Hungry as well. The wound in his neck hurt, and he thought it might break open and start bleeding.

Then one night they stopped and the prisoners were left tied, without food or water. The men piled up like dogs to sleep on the ground. They were woken up in the early hours of the morning by the Guards shining lamps in their faces, and were told to stand.

The leader of the Guards said, "We had a talk and decided that you animals are just wasting our time."

Then the Guards raised their guns. A boy, not much over twelve, fell to his knees and started crying. An old man, gray-headed, said, "You can't mean to kill us here."

One of the Guards put down his gun and looked at the leader and said, "I didn't join the Home Guard to kill grandpas and little boys."

The leader said to him, "Either you shoot them or you join them."

Inman looked off into the dark woods. "This is where I will die," he thought.

The firing started. Men and boys began falling all around. Veasey stepped forward and started shouting. He said, "It is not too late to stop this crime." Then he was shot a number of times. The bullet that hit Inman had already passed through Veasey's shoulder and as a result did not strike very hard. It hit Inman in the side of his head and came out behind his ear. He fell immediately but stayed partly conscious, unable to move or close his eyes. He watched as people died all around him and fell chained together.

When the firing was done, the Guards seemed unclear what to do next. Finally, one of the men said, "We'd better get them under ground." They did the job badly, just digging out a shallow hole and throwing the men in and covering them with dirt. When they had finished, they climbed onto their horses and rode away.

Inman had fallen with his face on his arm and he was able to breathe because the earth around him was so thin and loose. He lay half conscious for hours, with the smell of the dirt pulling him down. Dying there seemed easier than not. But before the dawn of day, wild pigs came from the woods, attracted by the smell, and they started digging up the earth. Inman found that he was staring into the face of one of these creatures.

"Get away," Inman said.

The animal moved back and looked at him, surprised. Inman sat up, his face covered in blood. He found the two holes in his head and felt them with his fingers. Then he started pulling at the rope with his hands, and Veasey appeared from the ground like a big fish, with his eyes open. Looking at him, Inman could not feel great sadness, but he did not feel glad either. By now, Inman guessed that he had seen thousands of men die. He feared his heart had been so touched by fire that he would never feel like an ordinary man again.

36

He looked around until he found a sharp stone and sat until sunrise rubbing his wrists against it. When he finally freed himself, he rolled Veasey over, face down. That was all he could do for him.

Inman set off walking west. All that morning he felt that his head would fall into a great number of pieces at his feet. By noon he came to a place where three roads met, and was unable to decide which one to take. He decided to sit by the side of the road and wait for a sign to show him which way he should go. After a time, he saw a yellow slave coming down the road driving a pair of bulls, one red and one white. They pulled a cart carrying a great number of green apples.

"God!" said the man, who was thin and strong. "What happened to you?"

He reached into the cart and threw a couple of apples to Inman, who ate them like a hungry dog. Then he looked up and said his thanks.

"Get on this cart and come with me," the yellow man said.

Inman climbed up and sat with his back against the side of the cart. When the yellow man came near the farm where he was owned, he made Inman lie down and covered him with apples. Then he took the cart into a barn and hid Inman under the roof.

Inman rested there for some days, spending the time sleeping and being fed by the slaves on fried corn and pieces of meat.

When his legs felt strong again, he prepared to set off on his journey once more. His clothes had been boiled clean and the slaves had given him an old black hat. There was a half-moon in the sky, and Inman stood at the door to say goodbye to the yellow man.

"You listen," the man said. "There are Federals everywhere around here. Which direction are you going?"

"West."

The yellow man gave Inman good directions, advising him to

go into the mountains in order to avoid the Feds. He gave him cornmeal and meat, and drew a detailed map for him.

Inman put his hands in his pockets for money to give the man. He wanted to be generous but found his pockets empty and remembered that his money was in the knapsack hidden in Junior's woodpile.

"I'd like to pay you but I've no money," Inman said.

"I don't think I'd take it anyway," the man said.

◆

Several nights later, Inman stood in front of Junior's house. He went to the back porch and found his knapsack in the pile of wood. He took his pistol out of the knapsack and the weight of it felt good in his hands.

Light was coming from the door of the barn, and Inman went to the door, opened it slightly and looked inside. Junior stood rubbing salt on some meat. Inman opened the door fully and Junior raised his face and looked up at him. Inman stepped to Junior and struck him across the face with his pistol and then hit him until he lay flat on his back, blood pouring from his nose and the cuts on his head.

Inman bent down and stared at Junior's face. The creature that lay on the ground was a horrible thing, but Inman feared that all men shared the same nature. He turned and went outside.

All that night he walked north. The yellow man was right, and horsemen passed again and again in the dark, but Inman could hear them coming in time to step into the bushes. When morning came there was fog, so he was able to light a fire in the woods and boil some meat and cornmeal. He stayed in the woods all day, sleeping and worrying when he heard the sound of horses, his mood as black as night.

Chapter 6   The Deserter's Story

One warm afternoon at the start of fall, Ruby and Ada were working in the lower field, which Ruby had planned as the winter garden. Some weeks earlier they had prepared the garden, plowing the earth and then planting tiny black seeds. The crops were growing well and Ada and Ruby were pleased with their progress.

They had been working among the plants for some time when they heard the sound of wheels and horses. A large cart came around the bend of the road and stopped by the fence. The cart was piled so full of things that the people all walked. Ada and Ruby went to the fence and saw a group of three women, half a dozen children, and two slaves. The women told them that they were from Tennessee and were on their way to South Carolina, where one of them had a sister. Their husbands were away fighting and they were escaping from the Federals in Tennessee. They asked if they could sleep in the barn.

While Ada took them to the barn, Ruby prepared a meal, killing three chickens and cooking them with boiled potatoes and beans. When supper was ready, the group came and sat at the dining room table and ate hungrily.

One of the women said, "That was good. For two weeks now we've had nothing to eat except dry corn bread."

"Why are you on the road?" Ada asked.

"The Federals came to our home and robbed even the slaves," the woman said. "They took every bit of food we had and all the jewelry we had hidden. Then they burned down our house in the rain and rode away. We had nothing, but we stayed for three days. Then we knew we had to leave."

The travelers went off to bed, and the next morning Ruby cooked nearly all the eggs they had and made a cake for the group. After breakfast, Ada drew a map of the area and sent the women on the next part of their journey.

Around noon, Ruby said she wanted to check the fruit trees, so Ada suggested that they have their lunch there. They made a picnic, and ate it on a blanket spread on the grass.

It was a sunny afternoon. Ruby examined the trees and decided that the apples were doing quite well. Then suddenly, she looked at Ada and said, "Point north." She smiled at the length of time it took Ada to work out which direction north was in. Such questions were a recent habit Ruby had developed. Ruby seemed to enjoy showing Ada how little she knew about the natural world. As they walked by the stream one day Ruby had asked, "Where does that water come from and where does it go?" Another day she had said, "Name me four plants on that hillside that you could eat." Ada did not yet have those answers, but she felt that she was learning. Now, as they sat on the blanket, she told Ruby that she envied her knowledge of how the world worked. "How did you learn these things?" Ada asked.

Ruby said she had learned the little she knew in the usual way. A lot of it was grandmother knowledge, learned from wandering around, talking to any old woman who would talk back, watching them work, and asking questions. Partly, though, she said that it was mostly a matter of careful observation.

They sat quietly for a time, and then in the warm, still air of the afternoon Ruby lay down and slept on the blanket. Ada was tired too but she fought off sleep like a child at bedtime. She rose and walked beyond the fruit trees to the edge of the wood, where the tall fall flowers grew, yellow and dark blue and gray. Birds flew among the flower heads. Ada stood still, watching the busy movements of insects. On a day like this, despite the war and the hard work the farm needed, she could not see how she could improve her world. It seemed so fine she doubted it could be done.

That evening, after Ruby had gone to bed, Ada remained on the porch looking out past the fields to the mountains and up to the darkening sky. Everything was becoming still. She remembered that she and Monroe had sat together on a night like this just after moving to the cove. Monroe had commented that the mountains were signs of another world, a world beyond our own that we deeply longed for. And Ada had then agreed.

But now, as she looked out at the view, she thought that this was no sign but was all the life there is. It was an opposite position to Monroe's, but still created its own powerful longing.

Ada left the porch and walked past the barn into the field. The sun was setting fast and the mountains were gray in the dying light. There was a great feeling of loneliness that Ada had felt in the place from the beginning. Monroe had had an explanation. He said that in their hearts people feel that long ago God was everywhere all the time; the sense of loneliness is what fills the emptiness when He leaves us.

It was cold. Ada went to put away Waldo, and as the cow rose to its feet, she felt its heat rise from the flattened grass around her legs. She bent and put her hands under the grass and into the dirt that still felt as warm as a living thing from the heat of the day and the body of the cow.

◆

They had begun walking to the town in the rain, Ada wearing a long coat and Ruby an enormous sweater that she had made. They carried umbrellas, but an hour later the rain had stopped and the weather had turned sunny. It was largely a pleasure trip that the two young women were taking, although they did need to buy a few small things. Mainly, though, after weeks of hard, back-breaking work, Ada longed to go on a trip to town and the morning's bad weather had not stopped her.

"I'm going to town if I have to get there on my hands and knees," she had said to Ruby.

In town, Ada and Ruby first walked about the streets, looking at

41

the stores, the carriages, and the women with their shopping baskets. The town was small and ordinary, with eleven stores, a church, and a courthouse—a white building set back from the road. There were deep tracks in the streets from the wheels of carts and carriages.

Ada and Ruby did their shopping, buying bullets, pencils, and a drawing book. For lunch they bought beer, hard cheese, and fresh bread and took it down by the river and sat on rocks to eat. Later, as they walked down the main street on the way out of town, they saw a group of people standing by the courthouse, looking up at a window. Joining the group, they found that a prisoner was talking to the people below.

He talked angrily and fast, claiming that he had fought hard in the war and had killed many Federals. He had been shot in the shoulder at Williamsburg. But he had recently stopped believing in the war, and since he had joined the army out of choice, his only crime was his decision to leave and walk home. Now here he was in prison. And they might hang him, though he had fought like a hero.

The prisoner then told the crowd that the Home Guard had taken him some days previously from his father's farm in the mountains. He had been hiding there with other outliers. It had been early evening when the outliers and the prisoner's father had heard the sound of horses approaching. His father took his gun and went out to the road, while the outliers ran to hide in the barn.

A small group of horsemen came slowly around the bend. There were two great dark men who looked like each other, and a thin white-headed boy wearing farm clothes. The fourth man looked like a traveling preacher in his long black coat and white shirt.

"Stop right there," the prisoner's father said to the horsemen when they were some distance away. They did not stop immediately but came closer.

The old man said to the man in the black coat, "I know who you are. You're Teague. Get over here."

Teague looked at the old man with dead eyes, and did not move. The other men got off their horses. Suddenly the white-headed boy fell down in the dirt and screamed. The old man turned to look at him, and as he did, one of the black men hit the old man hard on the head and then knocked his gun from his hand. The old man fell on his back, and the black man beat him with his gun until he lay still. Then he took his sword and stuck it into the old man's stomach.

The boy got up and stood over the man and looked at him. "He's ready to meet his Maker," he said.

Laughing, the four approached the house, walking around it three times before bursting through the front and back doors at the same moment. Within minutes they were out again, carrying a cooked chicken and two sacks of potatoes, which they put in their baskets.

Then, without a word, they went toward the barn. As they approached it, the door flew open and the three outliers ran out, holding farm tools as weapons. Teague put his gun to his shoulder and shot the first two men, who fell to the ground. The last man, the prisoner, stopped, dropped his weapon, and raised his hands.

Teague looked at him a minute, then said to the white-headed boy, "Birch, get me something to tie his hands and we'll lead him back to town on the end of a line."

The boy went to the horses and came back with some rope, but when they tried to tie the prisoner, he fought and screamed. Finally they managed to throw him to the ground and put his wrists and ankles together.

"He's a madman," Birch said.

They brought a chair from the house and tied the man into it.

"I'm thinking we should hang him from the top of the barn," Teague said.

"It'd look better if we brought someone into town now and then," Birch said.

The men talked for a while and decided that Birch was right. They tied the chair to the cart that stood in the yard, then fixed the cart to a horse, and set off for town.

By the time the prisoner had stopped talking, the sun had set, and Ruby and Ada turned from the courthouse and started walking home. For a time they were wordless with shock, but later they discussed the prisoner's story. Ada was not sure it was completely true, but Ruby said that it fitted what she knew of men's natures.

Chapter 7   Two Women

Inman followed the yellow man's map through what the people of the area called hill country. Nights were cool and the leaves were beginning to change color. There was too much open ground to feel good about walking by day, and by night the roads were so full of dark riders that Inman spent as much time hiding in bushes as walking. As soon as he could, Inman left the dangerous roads of the valleys and took a narrow path that aimed north toward the mountains. He climbed for part of one day and all of the next, and there was still a wall of mountain rising in front of him.

Late in the afternoon cold rain began falling, and it was past the middle of the night when he came to a big tree with a large hole in it. He climbed inside, glad to find a dry place, and fell asleep.

He woke soon after dawn, feeling tired, ill and stiff, with the wounds in his head and neck burning hot. All the food he had left in his knapsack was a cup of cornmeal, and it was too wet to make a fire. He sat for a time on a rock, and then got up and walked all morning through the dark woods. The path went up and up, and Inman had no idea where it was leading.

Near midday he came around a bend, and saw a tiny person leaning over a bush. When he came closer, he saw that it was a little old woman, who was putting food in a bird trap.

Inman stopped and said, "Hello, ma'am."

The little woman looked up at him. She was quite old, that was clear, but her cheeks were as pink and fine as a girl's. She wore a man's hat, and her thin white hair hung to her shoulders. Her full skirt and blouse were made of animal skins and she had a gun in her belt.

"I'm wondering if this road goes anywhere," Inman said.

"It goes west, I believe," the woman said.

"Thank you," said Inman.

The woman looked at Inman. "Those look like bullet holes in your head," she said. "You look faint. White."

"I'm fine," Inman said.

"You look like you could eat something. I'd be glad if you'd take shelter and dinner at my camp."

"Then I'd be a fool to say no," Inman said.

Inman followed the woman as she climbed to a bend, and from there they left the forest and walked on great rocks along the side of a mountain. A river gorge stretched blue and purple far below them. Then they entered a narrow path cut into the mountain and soon came to a dark cove with a little stream running through it. A small caravan stood in a space surrounded by trees. Birds walked on the roof of the caravan, whose sides were painted with colorful scenes, and plants had twisted themselves around the wheels.

The woman stopped and shouted, "Hey!" and about two dozen goats came out the woods, their yellow eyes bright and smart, the bells around their necks ringing. The woman disappeared around the side of the caravan and the goats followed her. Inman found her building up her cooking fire, and when it was burning well, Inman went to it and put out his hands to warm. A little brown and white goat came to the woman and she stroked it and scratched its neck until it lay down. Inman thought it was a peaceful scene. Then, with one smooth movement, she took a knife from her pocket and cut deep into the animal's neck. The little goat's body shook as she continued to stroke it until it lay still.

Inman watched the old woman as she cut the goat's body into pieces, some of which she put over the fire to cook. Other pieces she put in a pot with water and vegetables.

"By dinnertime we'll have a good meal," she said.

Later, the rain started again and Inman went into the caravan and sat by the tiny stove. There was a table piled high with papers and books and on the walls there were drawings of plants, some colored, with a great deal of tiny writing around the edges of the paper.

The woman fried some bread and gave it to Inman, together with some meat. "Thank you," said Inman, eating it fast. While he ate, she began making cheese from goat's milk. When she was finished, she handed him some of the milk. Then she sat in a chair by the stove and took her shoes off.

"Did you run off from the war?" she asked.

Inman showed her the angry cut at his neck. "Wounded and sent home," he said.

"Oh, I'm sure," she answered.

"How long have you been camped here?" asked Inman.

She thought for a minute. "Twenty-six years," she said.

"Never married?"

"Yes, I was, though I guess he's dead now. I was a stupid little girl and he was old. He'd already had three wives who'd all died. There was a boy I liked but this man had a nice farm and my family sold me to him. He treated me like a slave. I got up one night and rode away before dawn on his best horse. I've been alone since then. There's a little town about a half day's walk away. I sell cheese there and medicines that I make from plants."

She looked at him carefully. "Those new wounds in your head

are not so bad. When they heal up, the hair will cover them and no one will know they're there."

Then she said, "Listen, I don't care that you've run off from the war. It's dangerous for you, that's all."

He looked her in the eyes and saw that they were full of kindness. For a long time he had not met anyone who he trusted the way he did this goatwoman, so he told her what was in his heart. The shame he felt about shooting the Federals, men like him, who ran at guns and died. Then he told her how that morning he had found a bush of dusty blue berries. He had picked them and eaten them for breakfast and watched as some birds had flown across the sky toward the south. At least nature doesn't change, he thought. Inman had seen only change for four years, and guessed that people fought wars because they were bored. But sooner or later you get tired of watching people kill each other. So that morning he had looked at the berries and felt happy, knowing that nature continued unchanging.

The woman thought about what he had said, then got up and took a bottle containing a thick liquid from her cupboard. She went to Inman and rubbed the liquid on the wounds on his head and neck. When she had finished, she handed the bottle to him.

"Take it with you," she said. "Rub it on thick until it's gone. And take these too. Take one a day, starting now." She took some large pills from a purse and put them in his hand.

Sometime in the evening they ate the roast meat and the food in the pot. They sat side by side and listened to the faint rain come down in the woods. To Inman's surprise, he started talking about Ada, describing her character and her beauty, and his realization that he loved her and wanted to marry her. Then they sat for a time without talking while the rain came down harder.

"It must get cold in winter up here," Inman said.

"Cold enough. I keep the fire hot and the blankets deep, and I'm careful not to let my ink and paints freeze."

"What is it that you do in those books?" Inman asked.

"I draw pictures and write."

"About what?"

"Everything. The goats. Plants. Weather. I keep a record."

"And you've spent your life this way?"

"Until now, I have. I'm not dead yet."

"Don't you get lonely?"

"Sometimes, yes. But there's plenty of work."

The rain began falling harder and they stopped their talking, and Inman went on his hands and knees under the caravan, rolled up in his blankets, and slept. He rose at dawn and packed his things.

"I need to go," he told the old woman. "But I'd like to pay you for the food and medicine."

"You could try," the woman said. "But I wouldn't take it."

"Well, thank you," Inman said.

"Listen," the woman said. "If I had a boy, I'd tell him the same as I'm telling you. Watch out for yourself."

"I will," Inman said.

He turned to walk out of the caravan, but she stopped him. She said, "Here, take this with you," and she handed him a square of paper on which was drawn in great detail a branch of blue-purple berries.

♦

Inman wandered the mountains for days, lost in the fog and rain that never seemed to stop. He used the goatwoman's medicine until it was gone, and the wounds in his neck and head had healed. His knapsack became empty of food. At first he hunted, but without success. He tried fishing, but there were few fish in the mountain streams. He felt like a wild animal, almost mad with hunger. God, if I could grow wings and fly, he thought, I would be gone from this place. I'd fly far away and watch the world from a high rock.

Then, just as he thought that he could go no further, he came to a lonely little one-room cabin set above the road. The windows were pieces of paper. There was a pig making noises by the fence. Inman stepped up to the gate and shouted, and a young woman, a girl really, came to the door and looked out. She was a tight-skinned, pretty little thing, and wore a light cotton dress that did not suit the weather. She looked at him for a minute and then said, "Well, come in."

"I'll pay for what I eat," said Inman.

"I have very little, but I won't take money. There's cornbread and beans, that's all."

She turned and walked into the house. Inman followed. The room was dark, lit only by the fire, and though there was very little furniture the room was clean. A small baby lay warmly wrapped on the bed.

The woman pulled one of the chairs to the fire and pointed to Inman to sit, and in a minute a faint steam had begun to rise from his wet clothes. She served him a plate piled high with beans and bread. Inman started eating loudly and fast, while the woman sat watching him with some disgust.

"I'm sorry. I've not taken actual food in days," he said.

"There's no need to be sorry," she replied.

Inman looked at her closely for the first time. "How old are you?" he asked.

"Eighteen."

"Name's Inman. Yours?"

"Sara."

"Why are you here all alone?"

"My man, John, went off to the fighting. He died some months ago. They killed him up in Virginia. He never saw his baby, and it's just the two of us now."

Inman sat silent for a minute. "Do you have any help here?" he said.

49

"None."

"How do you manage?"

"I use a little plow to grow corn and vegetables. And there are a few chickens for the eggs. That pig is our food for the winter. I have to kill it soon, but I've never killed a pig before."

Listening to her, Inman thought that she would be old in five years' time. He saw all the world hanging over the girl like a trap, ready to drop and destroy her.

"I could help," he said.

"I couldn't ask it. I'd have to do it as an exchange. I could clean and sew up the holes in those clothes of yours. And you could put on clothes my man left. He was about as tall as you are."

She left the room and returned with a pile of folded clothes, a clean pair of good boots, and a bowl of water and soap. He stepped outside, took off his clothes, and washed himself. Then he dressed. The dead man's clothes fitted quite well, and the boots were perfect. When he went back indoors, he felt like the ghost of her husband.

They sat quietly by the fire for a time. Then she said, "You'll have to sleep in the henhouse."

He walked out and took his knapsack and went to the henhouse. It was almost freezing and he rolled himself in his wet blankets. He had only just fallen asleep when he was woken up by the girl.

"Come inside, please," she said. And she turned and walked away. When he went back inside she was in bed, her hair spread thick across her shoulders.

"If I asked you to lay in bed with me but not do anything else, could you do it?" she said.

Inman looked at her and wondered what she saw looking back. A stranger filling the clothes of her husband. "Yes," he said. He went over, pulled off his boots, and climbed under the bed covers. They both kept absolutely still. Then she started to cry, her chest shaking. After a time, she sat up and started talking about her husband. She just wanted Inman to listen to her story, and every time he tried to speak she silenced him. When she had finished talking, she reached out and touched the cut in Inman's neck. She rested her hand there for a moment before taking it away, then rolled over with her back to him and soon fell asleep. But tired as he was, Inman could not rest. A woman had not touched him like that for so long that he hardly saw himself as human. He saw his life now as a dark mistake and did not even think it possible to pull Sara to him and hold her close until daylight.

Inman was woken by Sara shaking his shoulder and saying urgently, "Get up and get out."

It was gray dawn and the cabin was freezing cold, and there was the faint sound of horses coming up the road.

"If it's the Home Guard, it would be better for both of us if you were not here."

Inman pulled on his boots and rushed out the back door to the line of trees beyond the stream. There, he hid behind a bush that gave him a view of the front of the house. He could see Sara run across to where the pig slept. She was driving the animal toward the woods when there was a call from down the road.

"Stop right there."

Blue jackets—Federals. Inman saw three men on horses, all carrying guns. One of the men went to her and told her to sit on the ground. The pig sat on the ground beside her. The other two men went into the house and there was the sound of things breaking. When the men reappeared, one of them carried the baby. It was crying, and Sara begged them to give her the child but they would not. Then Inman could hear that they were asking her about money, where she had it hidden. Sara told the truth, that she only had what they could see. They asked again and again, and then led her to the porch and tied her to it. One of the men took the baby's clothes off and lay the child on the frozen ground.

51

Inman could hear one of the men say, "We have all day," and then he could hear Sara scream.

The men searched the yard, hoping to find money or jewelry buried in the earth, but they found nothing. Then the leader walked to Sara and pointed his gun at her. "You really don't have anything, do you?"

One of the men gave the baby to her. Then they gathered up the chickens and hung them on their horses. When Sara saw the leader taking the pig away, she shouted, "That pig's all I have. Take it and you'll kill us both." But the men climbed on their horses and went down the road, leading the pig behind them on the end of a rope.

When they had disappeared, Inman ran to Sara. He said, "Warm up your baby and then build a fire as high as your head and put a big pot on to boil." And he ran down the road.

He followed the Federals, wondering what he intended to do. They did not go far before they built a fire and tied the pig to a tree. Then they killed two chickens and put them to roast on the fire.

Inman circled the area, and in the rocks near the camp he found a shallow cave. Returning to the edge of the men's camp, he climbed a big tree. In just a minute one of the men walked under the tree and stopped.

Inman said, "Hey!"

The man looked up and Inman shot him. The bullet entered at the shoulder and left through the stomach. The man fell to the ground immediately.

"Did you hit it?" one of the men in the camp called out.

Inman climbed down from the tree, circled the camp, hid behind a bush, and waited. Soon, the men went to find their friend. Inman followed them. Discovering that he was dead, they stood for a time and talked about what they ought to do. They decided to look for the killer. Inman followed them, moving nearer and nearer. When he shot them, he was so near he was almost touching them. They fell in a pile.

"If you'd stayed home, this wouldn't have happened," Inman said.

He dragged all three bodies to the cave and sat them up together. Then he led the horses far beyond the cave and shot them in the heads. It was not a happy thing to do, but he knew that if he left them free, people would come looking for their owners. Finally, he returned to the camp, picked up the cooked chickens, and led the pig back down the road.

When he returned to the cabin, Sara had built a good fire in the yard and there was a big pot of water boiling over it. They had an early lunch of the cooked chickens and then started work. Within two hours the pig had been killed, skinned, and cut into sections. They worked until dark, using all the parts of the pig and salting the meat.

Then they washed and went inside and Sara cooked.

After dinner, Sara said, "You'd look better if you shaved."

So Inman shaved in front of a metal mirror. The eyes that looked back at him had a look that he did not remember, a look that was more than just food hunger. It was a killer face, with eyes that looked at you sideways. But Inman tried to believe that this face was not him in any true way, and that it could in time be changed for a better one.

When he came back in, Sara smiled at him and said, "You look part human now."

They sat and looked at the fire and Sara held the baby in her lap. It would not sleep, so she sang it a song, a song which expressed such loneliness that it hurt Inman to hear it. The sound was of an old tired woman, and Sara was so young to sound that way. For the rest of the evening they hardly talked, but sat side by side in front of the fire, rested and happy, and later they again lay in bed together.

The next morning, Inman ate the brains of the pig before setting off on his journey again.

Chapter 8   Stobrod Returns

As the fall progressed, Ruby made plans for the coming winter. One afternoon, she threw two big sacks of apples over Ralph, the horse, and set off for town. She returned carrying six sacks of vegetables that she had exchanged for the apples. When she saw Ada, she handed her a letter, dirty as an old work glove. Ada recognized the handwriting but put the letter away, not wanting to read it while Ruby watched.

That evening, when Ruby had gone to bed, Ada sat on the porch and took the letter from her pocket. By now she had read it several times. She found parts of it hard to understand. Inman seemed to feel that there were strong feelings between them, although Ada could not say exactly how she felt. She had not seen Inman in almost four years, and it had been more than four months since she had last heard from him. The letter she held now was without date, and she did not know if it had been written a week ago or was three months old. He mentioned that he was wounded and talked about coming home, but did he mean now or at the end of the war?

She tried to read the letter in the dark. The only part she could see clearly was this short paragraph:

If you still possess the photograph of me that I sent four years ago, I ask you, please throw it away. I no longer look the same in any way.

Ada of course went immediately to her bedroom and opened drawers until she found the photograph. She had put it away because she had never thought it looked much like Inman. His expression in the picture was very serious, and didn't look like her memory of him on the last day before he left for the war.

54

He had come to the house to say goodbye. He was, at the time, living in a room in the town but planning to leave in two days, three at the most. They had walked together down to the stream beyond the fields. Inman, as they talked, was sometimes serious and sometimes cheerful. Ada found herself wondering, "What will I feel if he is killed?" But she could not, of course, say the thought aloud. She did not have to, though, because Inman at that moment said, "If I am shot to death, in five years you'll hardly remember my name."

"You know it's not that way," she said.

In her heart, though, she wondered, "Is anything remembered forever?" Inman looked away and seemed to be made shy by what he had said.

"Look there," he said. He looked up at Cold Mountain, which was wintery and gray. He started telling her a story about the mountain that he had heard from an old Indian woman. It was about a village called Kanuga that many years ago stood on the Pigeon River.

One day, a stranger had come into Kanuga and the people had fed him. As he ate, they asked him if he came from far away.

"No," he said, "I live in a town near here." He pointed in the direction of Cold Mountain.

"There is no village up there," the people said.

"Oh yes," the stranger said. "The Shining Rocks are the entrance to our country."

"But I've been to the Shining Rocks many times, and have seen no such country," said one man, and others agreed, because they knew the place he spoke of well.

"You must fast," the stranger said. "If not, we see you but you do not see us. Our land is not like yours. Here there is constant fighting and sickness. And soon an enemy will come and take your country away from you. But there we have peace. And although we die, as all men do, and must hunt for food, our minds are not filled with fear. I have come to invite you to live with us. But before you come, you must fast for seven days. Then climb to the Shining Rocks and they will open like a door, and you may enter our country and live with us."

Having said this, the stranger went away. After much discussion, the people decided to accept the invitation. They did not eat for seven days, all except for one man who, each night, secretly went to his house and ate meat.

On the morning of the seventh day, the people climbed toward the Shining Rocks, arriving at sunset. When the people stood in front of the white rocks, a cave opened like a door, and they saw that it was light inside, not dark. In the distance, inside the mountain, they could see a river and fields of corn. Then there was thunder and the sky turned black. The people were frightened, but only the man who had eaten the meat became really afraid. He gave a cry of terror and immediately the thunder stopped and the cave door closed, so that there was only the white rock, shining in the last light of the sun.

The people went sadly back to Kanuga. Soon, the stranger's words came true and their land was taken from them.

When Inman was finished, Ada said, "That was a strange story. You don't believe it, do you?"

She immediately regretted saying this, because the story obviously meant something to Inman. He looked at her and then at the stream. Then he said, "That old woman looked older than God and she cried tears when she told the story."

"But it can't be true," Ada said.

"I believe it's true that she had the chance to live in a better world and somehow she lost it."

Neither of them knew what to say next, so Inman said, "I need to go." He took Ada's hand and put his lips to the back of it, before letting it go. He had walked some distance before he turned around and saw Ada turning to walk to the house. Too soon. She had not even waited for him to pass the first bend in the road. Realizing what she had done, Ada stopped and looked at Inman.

Inman turned to face her and said, "You don't have to stand watching me."

"I know I don't," Ada said.

"You don't want to, I can see that."

"It wouldn't help," she said.

"It might make some men feel better." He took off his hat and raised it to her. "I'll see you when I see you," he said.

They walked away, this time without looking back.

That night, though, Ada did not feel happy about Inman going to war. It worried her that she had not cried or said what thousands of women said as men left, that they would wait for the man's return forever. She suspected that, out of habit, she had been distant and cold, and she feared that one day she would find that she could show no other feelings to the world.

She slept badly, her thoughts returning to Inman again and again. But when she woke the next morning, she felt clear-headed and bright, and decided to correct her mistake. The day was cloudless and warm. Ada told Monroe that she wanted to go into town and they drove off in the carriage. When they got there, Monroe gave her twenty dollars and told her to buy something nice. They separated and Ada bought a book and a scarf. Then, knowing it was not how a young lady should behave, she walked to the place where Inman was staying, and climbed the steps to his door.

Inman's face showed surprise when he saw Ada. He came out of his room and crossed his arms. There was a long silence.

She said, "I wanted to tell you that I thought things ended badly yesterday. Not at all as I wished them to be."

Inman's mouth tightened. He said, "I don't believe I understand you. I didn't expect anything different."

At Inman's reply, Ada thought about walking away and putting him forever behind her. But she said, "We might never speak again, and I know I disappointed you yesterday. I didn't follow my heart. I'm sorry for that."

"It's too late," Inman said, still standing with his arms crossed, and Ada reached out and pulled until she unlocked his arms. Then she took his wrist and held it.

Neither of them, for a moment, could look the other in the face. Then Inman pulled his hand away and threw his hat in the air and caught it. They both smiled, and Inman put one hand to Ada's waist and pulled her to him for the kiss they had not given each other the day before.

They walked together down the steps, feeling that a promise had been made.

"I hope I see you soon," Inman said.

"We both do, then," Ada replied.

♦

One afternoon, as Ruby was working in the yard, she saw a man in dark clothes and a big gray hat coming toward her, with a smile on his face.

"So you're not dead?" Ruby said.

"Not yet," said Stobrod.

Ruby looked at him. He had changed. He seemed such an old, small man, with his hair half gone from his head.

"How old are you now?" she said.

He thought for a minute. "Maybe forty-five," he said.

"You've run off from the fighting, no doubt."

"I fought like a hero."

"You sit on the porch steps and I'll bring you some food," Ruby said.

She went inside and found Ada sitting by the window in the kitchen.

"My daddy's out on the porch," Ruby said.

"Pardon?"

"Stobrod. He's come home from the war. But I don't care. A plate of food and then we'll send him away."

Ruby put some food on a plate and carried it out to the table underneath the apple tree.

"He could eat in here," Ada said.

"No," Ruby said.

They watched from the window as Stobrod ate, then Ruby went out to collect his plate.

"Have you somewhere to go?" she asked.

Stobrod told her that he was living with a group of outliers in a deep cave in the mountains. They wished only to hunt and eat, get drunk, and make music.

"Well, I guess that suits you," said Ruby.

She waved at him to leave and he walked off, in the direction of Cold Mountain.

The two women did not think that they would see Stobrod again, but the next evening, as they were having supper at the table under the apple tree, Stobrod and another man came out from the woods.

"You just say, and I'll send them on their way," Ruby said.

Ada said, "We have plenty."

The two men sat down and Ruby handed them food, which they ate fast. At first, Ruby refused to speak, and Stobrod talked about the war with Ada, saying how he hoped it would end so he could come down from the mountain.

"It's no joke living on the mountain," Stobrod said. "That Teague and his men are killers."

"Who's your friend?" Ruby asked Stobrod.

"That's Pangle. He's not very smart."

Pangle was a soft, fat thing, with a big round head and hair that was almost white. He had no talent in the world, except a recently discovered ability to play the fiddle, but he was gentle and kind and looked on everything that happened with soft, wide eyes.

When supper was done, Stobrod lifted his sack off the ground and took a fiddle from it. He told the women that something about the war had completely changed how he felt about music.

"Some say I fiddle now like a man wild with fever," he said. He told them how, in January 1862, a man had come into the army camp, asking for a fiddler. The man's fifteen-year-old daughter was dying, and the girl had asked for fiddle music to be played to help the pain.

Stobrod had picked up his instrument and followed the man to his house. He had played some dance tunes to the girl as she lay dying, and when he had finished she had asked him to play something of his own. Stobrod was surprised by this request and sat thinking for a minute. Then he started playing, and was surprised by the sad, beautiful sound that came from the fiddle.

When he was done, the girl looked at him and said, "That was fine." And then she turned her face away and died.

Since then, music had become more and more important to Stobrod. He lost all interest in the war, and instead spent his time learning new tunes from other fiddlers, and making up his own. By now he knew nine hundred fiddle tunes, many of which he had written himself.

"Well, play then," Ruby said.

Stobrod sat and thought for a minute, then started to play. The tune was slow and sad, quite difficult to play, and very beautiful. Ruby and Ada listened in surprise. To Ada, Stobrod's playing seemed to show that even a man like Ruby's father could learn and change for the better.

When Stobrod had finished, he played other wild and beautiful tunes of his own, and Pangle took his fiddle and played with him. As the last tune came to an end, Stobrod smiled a deep, long smile of silent joy.

"He's done you some good there," Pangle said to Ada. And then he seemed shocked that he had spoken directly to her, and put his head down, and then looked off into the woods.

Stobrod said, "I want to ask you something."

"What?" Ruby said.

"The problem is, I need help. I'm frightened."

He explained that the group of outliers he was living with had started robbing farms. He was afraid that they would attract the attention of the law, and that the Home Guard would come for them. Stobrod had decided to leave the group, taking Pangle, who was one of the group, with him. He needed a promise of food, a place like the barn to stay in in bad weather, and maybe now and then a little money.

"Eat roots," said Ruby. "Drink muddy water."

"Have you not got more feeling than that for your daddy?" Stobrod said.

"When I was not yet eight, you left me to look after myself for three months. And there's this. If the stories about Teague are even half true, we have plenty to worry about if we shelter you. This is not my place. But if it was, I'd say no."

And with that, Ruby rose and walked off into the darkness.

Sometime later, having sent Stobrod off with half-promises of food, Ada was sitting out on the porch, looking at the moon, which was full and high and throwing such light that every tree had a blue shadow. She thought about a love song that Stobrod had sung that night. Its last line was: "Come back to me is my request." Stobrod had sung the line with feeling, and Ada had to admit that, at least now and then, it was important to say what your heart felt, straight and simple. She had never been able to do it in her whole life, but she thought that she would try now.

She went into the house and came back with pen, ink, and paper, then stared at the paper for some minutes. None of the words that came into her head seemed real. Finally she wrote,

"Come back to me is my request." She signed her name and folded the paper and addressed it to the hospital in the capital. Then she wrapped herself tight in the blankets, and soon she was asleep.

Chapter 9   Death in the Mountains

If the part of the mountain they climbed had a name, Stobrod did not know it. He and the two men with him walked looking down at the ground, their hats pulled over their noses, and their hands pulled up into their coat sleeves to protect them from the cold. The Pangle boy was close behind Stobrod, and the third figure followed six steps back. The night before, they had found a couple of dead rabbits and had lit a fire and cooked and eaten them. Now they regretted it, because they all had bad stomach pains, and from time to time one of them had to go off behind a bush.

It was almost dawn and there was no color to anything, only shades of brown and gray. They came to a piece of flat ground where three paths met. The three men stood together, breathless from the climb.

"It's cold," the third man said. He had been one of the group at the outliers' cave and had never offered a name. He was from Georgia, a boy of no more than seventeen years, black-haired, brown-skinned. He had fought in the war for a year, then left to walk back home. It had taken him three months to reach Cold Mountain, and he had been found by one of the outliers, wandering aimlessly in the forest. The men had agreed that he should leave with Stobrod and Pangle, who were setting off alone to find a cave to live in somewhere near the Shining Rocks.

First, however, they had gone to a hiding place where Ruby had hidden some food. Stobrod had told the boy about Ada and Ruby, and how Ada had persuaded Ruby to feed them, although the women could not give quite enough for the men to live on. Ruby would not allow the men to visit the farm, as she thought it was too dangerous, so she left the food in a place that she had discovered as a child. They had gone there before they started on their journey and found cornmeal, dried apple, and some meat and beans.

"Do you know which path we want?" the Georgia boy said now to Stobrod. But Stobrod was not at all sure where they were nor which way they were going.

Pangle watched him for some minutes, and then, apologizing, said he knew exactly where he was, and that the right-hand path went right across the mountain and was the path they wanted.

"We'll cook a meal and go on then," Stobrod said.

The men built a small fire and boiled up some cornmeal. They sat as near to the flames as they could, and passed a bottle, waiting for the fire and drink to warm them up. The Georgia boy sat bent over, with a hand on his stomach.

"If I'd known I'd feel this bad, I wouldn't have eaten one mouthful of that rabbit," he said.

He stood and walked slowly into the trees. Stobrod's head fell sleepily to his chest, and when he looked up again he was looking at three men on horses, their guns pointing at him. Stobrod started to get up.

"Sit still," Teague said. "I'm not even going to ask you if you have papers. We're looking for a group of outliers living in a cave. They've been robbing farms. If a man knew where that cave was, it might help him."

"I don't exactly know," Stobrod said. "I'd say if I did." His voice was quick and bright, but inside he was thinking that in a month he'd be back in Virginia using a gun.

Pangle looked in surprise at Stobrod. "That's not true," he said. "You know exactly where it is." And he gave a detailed description of how to find the cave.

"Thanks," Teague said and smiled at his men, and they all climbed off their horses. "We'll join you at your fire and take breakfast with you."

They built up the fire and sat around it like friends. The Guards had meat with them, and they cooked and ate it, offering some to the outliers. Teague took a bottle from his coat and handed it around. When they had finished eating, Teague looked at the fiddles, which were lying on the ground, and said, "Can you play those things?"

"A bit," Stobrod said.

"Play me something, then," Teague said.

Stobrod did not much want to. He was tired and he guessed that his audience did not take pleasure from music. But he picked up his fiddle and started to play, and Pangle joined him. Teague and his men had never before heard such strange, wild music, nor heard anyone play with such feeling and skill.

When they had finished, Birch said to Teague, "Good God, these are strange men."

Teague looked off into the distance. He stood and straightened his coat, then he took his gun and pointed it at the two men.

"Stand up against that big tree," he said.

The two men went and stood against it, holding their fiddles in front of them. Pangle put his free arm around Stobrod's shoulders. The Guards raised their guns and Pangle gave them a friendly smile.

"I can't shoot a man who's smiling at me," one of the men said.

"Stop smiling," Teague said to Pangle.

Pangle tried to stop smiling, but without success.

"Take your hat off and hold it over your face," Teague said.

Pangle raised his hat and put it over his face, and when he did the Guards fired. Pieces of wood flew from the tree trunk, where the bullets struck after passing through the meat of the two men.

64

"And when they had finished, they didn't cover them or even go and stand over them to say words. They just got on their horses and rode off. I don't know what kind of place this is, where people kill each other that way."

The Georgia boy sounded like someone who had had a terrible shock. "I saw it all," he said, "saw it all."

"Then why were you not killed or taken, if you were close enough to witness?" Ada said.

The boy thought about it. "I heard what I didn't see, anyway," he answered. "I'd stepped into the woods. I needed to be private."

"We get your meaning," Ruby said.

"I came here as fast as I could. I remembered where the fiddler said you lived."

"How long ago?" Ruby asked.

The boy thought for a moment. "Six or seven hours."

"You can guide us back there," Ada said.

But the boy did not wish to go back up the mountain, and would, he claimed, rather be shot where he stood than visit it again.

Ruby said, "Do as you want. We have no need of you. I know the place you're talking of. We'll feed you, though."

She opened the gate and let the boy into the yard. Ada stepped to her side and looked at her face, then reached out and touched the dark hair at Ruby's neck. But Ruby twisted her neck away and did not cry or show any sign of sadness. She expressed only one concern. Should they bury the men on the mountain or bring them to Black Cove?

"We can't just go up there and dig a hole," Ada said.

"If it was me, I'd rather rest on the mountain than anywhere else," said Ruby.

Ada could find no argument to that. She reached out and put

65

her arms around Ruby for comfort, if nothing else, but Ruby just stood with her arms by her sides.

The women made food for the boy, then started planning their journey. They packed blankets and shovels, cooking pots, matches, rope, a gun, lamps, and grain for the horse. Ruby decided that pants were more practical and they found two pairs of heavy wool hunting pants. They put on wool shirts and sweaters and big hats. Then they gave the boy food and blankets and told him to sleep in the barn until dark made it safe for him to travel. When they left leading the horse, the boy waved to them like a host saying goodbye to his guests.

Toward evening, snow fell through fog in the woods. Ada and Ruby walked under the trees, faint shapes moving through a place that had no color except shades of gray and black. They had climbed for a long time and were now going down into a valley. Light snow was falling and for a time they walked by a stream, but then the path they were following turned back into the forest. They walked on past sunset, and the snow started falling harder.

In time they came to an area with great flat rocks. Ruby looked around until she found the place that she was looking for, one that she had known as a child, where three rocks had fallen together to make a natural shelter. There was a little stream twenty meters away. The women gathered the driest wood they could find, made a fire at the entrance to the shelter, and boiled a pot of water for tea. Then they sat and drank it, and ate a few dried apples and dry bread.

The temperature was dropping fast, but the fire soon heated the stones, and when Ada and Ruby wrapped themselves in blankets and buried themselves among the dry leaves, they were warm as lying in a bed at home. "This is fine," Ada thought, as she lay there. She watched the fire shadows and listened to the sound of snow in the leaves and soon she slept a dreamless sleep, not even waking when Ruby rose to put more wood on the fire.

Next morning, they found the Pangle boy lying alone beneath the big tree, covered in snow. Ruby brushed away the snow to look at his face, and when she did she saw that he was still smiling. She put her hand to his fat cheek and then touched her fingers to his forehead.

Ada turned from him. "Where is he?" she said.

"No man from Georgia can tell more than half the truth," Ruby said. "Dead or alive, they took him with them."

They started digging a deep hole, and soon they were so hot in their coats that they had to take them off. When the hole was deep enough, they went to Pangle and each took a leg and slid him into the grave. By the time they had covered him, Ada was crying, though she had seen the boy only once in life. She made a cross from two thin branches and stood it in the soft ground at Pangle's head, and though she did not say words aloud over him, she said some in her mind. Then she went through the woods to the stream and knelt and washed her hands and face. She looked around and saw a low rock that formed a kind of shelter. Under it sat Stobrod, his eyes closed and his legs crossed, with his fiddle in his lap.

"Ruby," Ada called. "Ruby, I need you here."

They stood over him and his face was the color of the snow, since he had lost a great deal of blood. Such a little man. Ruby put her ear to his chest and listened.

"He's alive," she said.

She took off his clothes and found he had been hit three times. The most serious wound was a bullet that had gone through his chest into his back. Stobrod remained unconscious while Ruby lit a match and held a knife in the flame. Then she cut into Stobrod's back and he still made no sound as she put a finger around the bullet and pulled it out.

"You boil some water," Ruby said to Ada.

She wandered off through the woods, returning an hour later with roots she had found that she thought could be useful. She cut them up and packed them around Stobrod's wounds, holding them there with pieces of blanket.

After a time, she said, "It's too far home. He won't get there alive. And last night's shelter is too small for all of us. There's a place I know. If it's still there."

They carried Stobrod across the stream in blankets and laid him over the horse, then set off, the sky flat and gray above them. They walked for some time without speaking, except when Ruby said "Here," and then they turned. After some hours, they started going down into a valley, moving toward a stream that they could hear but not see. Ada began to see shapes through the trees. Cabins. A tiny Cherokee village, a ghost town, its people forced to leave by their enemies. Ada thought of Inman's story. She wondered if any of those who had lived in the village were still alive, and if they remembered this lonely place.

Ruby chose the best of the cabins and they took Stobrod off the horse and lay him on the dusty floor. The house had one windowless room and the rich smell of a thousand old campfires. While Ruby built a fire, Ada looked after the horse, which was wet and shaking. She looked at him and at the sky and thought that he might be dead on the ground by morning. She tried to lead him into the cabin but he did not want to go, and finally she used a big stick and hit him with it until he went in.

It was almost dark and Ada felt tired and cold and frightened. This seemed like the loneliest place on earth. Ruby had cooked some cornmeal, but Ada could not eat it. She sat with it in her lap, exhausted and silent. Outside, the snow started to fall again.

Chapter 10   The Meeting

When Inman was only a day's journey away from Black Cove, he stopped at a stream to wash himself and his clothes. He built a fire and spread the clothes on bushes near the fire to dry. He hoped to see Ada soon. He had imagined the scene many times, had seen himself walking up the road into Black Cove, exhausted, but with his courage and strength written on his face. He would be washed and in a clean suit. Ada would step out the door dressed in her fine clothes and would know him immediately. She would run to him, rushing across the yard, and then they would hold each other.

He had seen it in his mind so often that he was now unable to imagine it any other way. He found his way to Black Cove, taking care not to follow the road until he was near the house.

When he came to it, there was smoke from the chimney but no other sign of life. He knocked at the front door again but no one came. Then he went to the back door and knocked, and eventually an upstairs window opened and a black-haired boy asked him who he was and what he wanted.

In time, Inman persuaded the Georgia boy to let him in. They sat by the fire and Inman heard the story of the killings. The boy gave him the best directions he could and Inman set off again, walking up the mountain.

When he reached the place where three paths came together, there was hardly enough light for Inman to study the ground and see what story it told. There was black blood beneath a big tree where killing had been done. There had been a recent fire, and tracks led to a cross of sticks standing at the head of a hole that had been filled in.

Inman was puzzled, because he knew that two men had been buried there, but it seemed that only one had been. There were pieces of root on the ground and he picked them up and smelled them. He looked to where the tracks led, but he could not see far before they started disappearing in the dark. So he went and sat on a rock and listened to the stream, and tried to invent a story that would explain why the two women had gone on across the mountain instead of going back home.

But it was hard to think in the state he was in. For two days, Inman had not eaten. He looked at the roots on the ground and thought about eating them, but then he picked them up and threw them into the stream. He intended to fast until he found Ada. If she would not have him, he would go on to the heights and see if the doors of the Shining Rocks would open to him. Inman could think of no reason to hesitate. He would walk right out of this world and keep on going into that happy valley the old Cherokee Indian woman had described.

Inman lit a fire and rolled two large stones into it to heat. For a long time he lay wrapped in his blankets with his feet to the fire. His thoughts came and went and he had no control over them. Inman was afraid that he was falling apart at a bad time. He had hoped that Ada might save him from his troubles and the bad things he had done in the last four years. But a dark voice came into his mind and said that it didn't matter how much you wished for something and prayed for it, you would never get it. You could be far too ruined, with fear and hate eating your heart so that you were ready for your hole in the ground. But another part of Inman knew that there were tracks in the snow, and that if he woke up on one more day he would follow them wherever they led.

The fire began to die out, and he rolled the hot stones onto the ground and stretched out next to them and fell asleep. The cold woke him before dawn, and he set off to follow the tracks, although by now they were very faint. Then snow started falling again and they started to disappear. Inman began to run. But soon they had gone completely and Inman stopped in a place where the only sound was of snow falling on snow. He thought that if he lay down the snow would cover him, and when it melted it would wash the tears from his eyes.

♦

Ada and Ruby slept until Stobrod began coughing. Ruby went to him and his eyes opened, but he did not seem to know her. She put her hand to his forehead and said, "He's burning. Get some water and I'll put some fresh roots on his wound."

Ada took the pot to the stream and filled it full of water, and gave some of it to the horse. As she returned to the cabin, she saw that there were a dozen wild turkeys among the leafless trees of the hillside. She went in and put the pot by the fire. Stobrod lay quiet.

"There are turkeys on the hillside," she said.

"The gun's over there. Go kill us one," Ruby said.

"I've never fired a gun," said Ada.

"It's easy." Ruby picked up the gun and showed Ada how to use it. Ada looked doubtful and Ruby said, "The worst you can do is fail to kill a turkey, and we've all done that. Go on."

Ada followed the birds for some time, climbing when they climbed and stopping when they stopped. As she walked, she tried to be quiet and still in her movements. She did not take her eyes off them and eventually she got to the distance from them that Ruby had advised. She stood quietly and still they did not see her. Then she raised the gun slowly and fired, and to her surprise a pair fell. When Ada reached the fallen birds, she found that one was male and one female, and that their feathers shone like metal.

◆

Inman heard a shot near where he stood. He took his gun and went forward, holding it loosely in his hand. The light was low and snow was falling and had covered the branches of the trees. He walked down into a path, and at the end he seemed to see a figure, and when it saw him it pointed a gun at him.

A hunter, Inman guessed. He called out, saying, "I'm lost," and stepped forward slowly. First he could see the turkeys laid on the ground. Then he could see Ada's fine face on top of a strange figure wearing pants.

71

"Ada Monroe?" Inman said. "Ada?"

She did not answer but just looked at him, confused, and lowered the gun. She examined him and did not know him. His face was so thin above the beard, and he stared at her out of strange black eyes shining deep under the shadow of his hat. But Inman looked her in the eyes and knew it was Ada and felt love ringing in his soul.

"I've been coming to you on a hard road and I'm not letting you go," he said. But something in him would not let him step forward to hold her. He held out his empty hands.

Ada still did not know him. He seemed a madman, wandering in the storm, knapsack on his back, snow in his beard. She raised her gun again.

"I do not know you," she said.

When Inman heard the words, he thought, "Four years at war, but back now on home ground and I'm no better than a stranger here. This is the price I pay for the last four years."

"I believe I have made a mistake," he said.

He turned to walk away, to go on up to the Shining Rocks and see if they would have him. But there was no path to follow, just trees and snow and his own steps filling fast. He turned back to her and held out his empty hands again and said, "If I knew where to go, I'd go there."

Perhaps it was something about his voice, or the angle of his face. But suddenly Ada knew him. She lowered the gun and said his name and he said yes.

Now Ada looked at his face and saw not a madman but Inman. He was exhausted and thin, but still Inman. There was hunger written on his forehead, like a shadow over him. He needed food, warmth, kindness. In his eyes she could see that the long war and the hard road home had left his mind and heart half dead. Tears came to her eyes and she rubbed them away.

"You come with me," she said.

She picked up the turkeys by their feet and walked off carrying the gun on her shoulder. Inman followed and he was so tired he did not even think to offer to carry the turkeys for her. As they walked, Ada talked to Inman in the voice she had heard Ruby use to speak to the horse when it was nervous. The words did not matter. So she talked of the first thing that came to her, describing the village below and saying that it looked like a famous picture that she had seen on her travels with Monroe.

Inman was too tired to understand what she said. He only knew that she seemed to know her destination and that something in her voice said, "This minute, I know more than you do, and I know that everything might be fine."

Chapter 11   A Time to Love

The cabin was hot and bright from the fire, and with the door shut it was hard to say if it was morning or night outside. Ruby had made coffee. Ada and Inman sat drinking it, so close to the fire that the melted snow in their coats steamed around them. Nobody said much and the place seemed tiny with four people in it.

Stobrod moved his head from side to side. His eyes had a look of confusion and hurt in them. Then he lay still again.

Tired and warm from the fire, Inman could not keep his eyes open. There were so many things he wanted, but the first thing he needed was sleep. Ada folded a blanket and put it on the floor. She led him to it and he stretched out and fell asleep fully clothed.

While Inman and Stobrod slept, the snow fell and fell, and the two women spent a cold and almost wordless hour collecting wood and cleaning out another of the cabins. They built a hot fire in it, then cleaned the turkeys, put them on the end of long sticks, and roasted them all day over a slow fire. For a long time they sat close to the fire together and neither of them spoke.

Night came, and Ruby said, "I was watching you this morning with him and I've been thinking."

'What?' Ada asked.

"We're just starting. I've got a picture in my mind of how that cove needs to be. It will take a long time but I know how to get there. War or peace, there's nothing we can't do ourselves. You don't need him."

"I know I don't need him," Ada said. "But I think I want him."

"Well, that's different."

Ada paused, thinking hard. She knew that Inman had been alone too long, an outlier without the comfort of a human touch, a loving hand laid soft and warm on his shoulder, back, leg. And she too was lonely.

Finally she said aloud, "I don't want to find myself someday in a new century, an old bitter woman looking back, knowing that I hadn't had the courage to follow my heart."

◆

It was after dark when Inman woke. The fire had burned low and there was no way to tell what time of night it was. He turned and saw Stobrod, his eyes black and shining in the light. Stobrod looked at Inman and said, "Any water?"

Inman could not see any in the room so he rose. "I'll get you a drink," he said.

He stepped outside, and when he could see enough to walk, he went down to the stream and filled his bottle with water. He could see firelight shining yellow from the cabin where he had slept. And also from another, further down the stream. He smelled meat cooking and felt suddenly very hungry.

He went back inside and raised Stobrod and slowly poured water into his mouth. Then he built the fire up and, leaving Stobrod asleep, he walked down to the other lighted cabin.

"Hello," Inman said, and Ruby came to the door and looked

out. "I woke up," Inman said. "I don't know how long I was asleep."

"You've slept twelve hours or more," Ruby said, and moved so that he could come in.

Ada sat cross-legged on the ground beside the fire, and as Inman entered she looked up at him. Her dark hair was loose on her shoulders and Inman thought her as beautiful a sight as men are allowed to see. He did not know what to with himself, but thought that he would go and sit beside her.

Then Ada rose and did a thing he knew he would never forget. She reached behind him and put one hand on his back, at his waist. The other she pressed against his stomach.

"You feel so thin between my hands," she said.

Inman could think of no answer that suited the moment.

Ada took her hands away and said, "When did you last eat?"

Inman counted back. "Three days," he said. "Or four."

"Well then, you must be hungry."

Ada sat him down by the fire and gave him a plate of turkey with fried apple rings. Inman started eating hungrily, but then he stopped and said, "Are you not having any?"

"We ate some time ago," Ada said.

Ruby picked up a pot of soup and stood up, saying, "I'll see if I can get him to take some of this. And I'm going to clean that wound and sit with him for a time."

After Ruby left, neither Inman nor Ada could think of anything much to say. Inman began commenting on the food, but then he stopped and felt foolish. He wanted to lie on the blankets with Ada beside him and hold her close. He knew that it had taken all her courage to touch him as she had. Now he had to find a way to say what he had to say.

He went and sat behind her, then reached around her and pressed the inside of his wrists and arms against her shoulders.

"Did you write me letters while I was in the hospital?" he said.

"Several," she said. "But I did not know you were there until you were gone. So the first two letters went to Virginia."

"Tell me what they were about," he said.

Ada described them, and Inman said, "I'd love to have read them." He held his hands to the fire and said, "Twenty-six years since a fire was lit here."

This gave them a topic, and they sat for a time talking about the Cherokee village, imagining the lives that had been lived in that place. When they had finished, they sat quietly, and then Inman told Ada how, all the way home, his only hope was that she would have him, would marry him. But now, he said, he could not ask her to do so. Not to a man as ruined as he was.

"I'm ruined beyond repair, I fear," he said.

Ada turned and looked at him over her shoulder. She could see the white wound at his neck, and there were other wounds in the look of his face and in his eyes, which could not quite meet hers.

She turned back. She knew that cures of all sorts exist in the natural world. Even the most hidden root had a use. She had learned this, at least, from Ruby.

Without looking at him, she said, "I know people can be healed. Not all, but some can be. Why not you?"

"Why not me?" said Inman, testing the thought. He reached to Ada's dark hair, which lay loose on her back, and lifted it. Leaning forward, he touched his lips to the back of her neck and kissed the top of her head. Then he leaned back and pulled her against him, her waist into his stomach, her shoulders into his chest.

He held her tight and words poured out of him. He told her about the first time he had looked on the back of her neck as she sat in church. Of the feeling that had never let go of him since. He talked of the wasted years between then and now, and how you never get back the things you have lost. They will always stay lost. You can only choose to go on or not, and if you go on, you carry your wounds with you. But during all those wasted years, he had

76

had the wish to kiss her there at the back of her neck, and now he had done it.

Ada knew that Inman was trying to thank her for the touch she had given him when he entered the cabin. She lifted her hair from her shoulders and put her head slightly forward.

"Do that once more," she said.

But there was a sound at the door and Ruby came in, and saw the two looking uncomfortable. Nobody said anything.

"His fever's down now," Ruby said finally.

Inman returned to the other cabin to sleep. As he lay there, he tried to decide which part of the evening he had enjoyed most, Ada's hand on his stomach or her request just before Ruby opened the door. He was still trying to decide when he fell asleep.

The next day was gray and even colder, with snow falling soft and fine. They all slept late, and Inman took breakfast in the women's hut. Then, later in the morning, Ada and Inman fed and watered the horse and went hunting together. They walked up the hill and found nothing moving in the woods, not even animal tracks in the snow. Eventually, they came to a flat rock, and Inman brushed the snow from it, and they sat cross-legged facing each other, knee to knee.

Ada began talking. She wanted to tell how she had become what she was. They were different people now. He needed to know that. She told of Monroe's death, and about deciding not to return to Charleston, and all about Ruby. About weather and animals and plants and the things that she was starting to know. She still missed Monroe more than she could say, and she told Inman many wonderful things about him. But she told as well one terrible thing: that he had tried to keep her a child, and that he had mostly succeeded.

"And there's something you need to know about Ruby," Ada said. "Whatever happens between you and me, I want her to stay in Black Cove as long as she wants. If she never leaves, I'll be glad."

"Could she learn to accept me? That's the question," Inman said.

"I think she can," Ada said. "If you understand she is not a servant but my friend."

They returned to the village that afternoon carrying only wood for the fire. They found Ruby sitting by Stobrod. He seemed to know Ruby and Ada, but he was frightened of Inman.

"Who's that big, dark man?" he said.

Ruby wet a cloth and cleaned his face, and when she was done he immediately fell asleep. Ada looked at Inman, the tiredness in his face. She said, "I believe you ought to do the same."

"Just don't let me sleep past dark," Inman said. He went out and returned a minute later with a pile of wood for the fire. Then he left and the two women built the fire up and sat together for a long time with their backs against the cabin wall, a blanket around them. Then they slept, and when they woke it was almost dark. Ruby went to check Stobrod.

"His fever's up again," she said. "He'll stay or go, but tonight will decide. I'd better not leave him."

Ada came over and felt Stobrod's forehead. It did not feel too hot to her. She looked at Ruby but Ruby would not look back.

It was dark when Ada walked down the stream to the other cabin. She opened the door quietly and entered. Inman lay asleep and did not move. The fire had burned low. Ada took off her coat and put three branches on the fire, then went to Inman and knelt beside him. She touched his forehead and stroked his hair. He woke slowly, turning to look at her, but then his eyes closed and he slept again.

The world was such a terribly lonely place, and the only cure seemed to be to lie down beside him, skin to skin. Ada felt very frightened, but she put the fear away from her and started undoing the buttons on her pants. They were almost off when she looked towards Inman and found his eyes open, watching her.

"Turn your back," she said.

"Not for all the gold dollars in the world," Inman said.

She turned away from him, nervous and uncomfortable. But he leaned forward and pulled the clothes from her hands, and pulled her to him. Gently, he moved his hands up and down her, then pressed his forehead to her soft stomach and kissed her there. He pulled her against him and held her and held her. She put a hand to the back of his neck and pulled him harder, and then she pressed her white arms against him. And for a time that night, the cabin was a place that held within its walls no pain or even a faint memory of pain.

Later, Ada and Inman lay holding each other as the branches smoked in the fire and the snow whispered as it fell. And they did what lovers often do when they think the future stretches endlessly before them; they talked of the past, through most of the night, describing their childhood and youth in great detail. When they reached the war years, Inman only described them very generally and said little about himself.

"Then tell me of your long journey home," Ada said.

Inman thought about it, but then he let himself imagine that he had at last reached the end of his troubles. He had no wish to revisit them, so he told only of how on his journey he had watched the nights of the moon and counted them to twenty-eight and then started all over again.

Then he added, "I met a number of people on the way. There was a goatswoman that fed me."

They turned to the future and started talking about their plans. They imagined their marriage, the years passing happy and peaceful, with Black Cove organized according to Ruby's plans. Ada described these plans in detail and the only thing Inman requested was that they should keep a few goats. In fall the apple trees would be bright and heavy with apples and they would hunt birds together, and in summer they would catch fish. They were both at the age when they could think in one part of their minds that their whole lives stretched in front of them. At the same time another part guessed that their youth was almost finished for them and that a very different country lay ahead.

Chapter 12   The Last Goodbye

By the morning of the third day in the village, the sky had cleared and there was bright sun. The snow began to melt, dropping from the bent branches of trees, and all day there was the sound of water running under the snow on the ground. That evening the moon was full and its bright light threw shadows of tree trunks on the snow.

Ada and Inman lay under the covers for some time, talking, with the fire low and the door to the cabin open, letting a bar of cold moonlight shine onto their bed. They made a plan for themselves and discussed it for much of the night. They felt certain that the South was going to lose the war, which could not go on many more months. It certainly would not continue past late summer. The choices were these. Inman could return to the army. He would immediately be sent back to Petersburg, where he would try not to get killed and hope for an early end to the war. Or he could stay hidden in the mountains or in Black Cove as an outlier and be hunted like a wild animal. Or he could cross the mountains north and give himself up to the Federals. They would make him sign a document saying he was loyal to their cause, but then he could wait for the fighting to end and come home.

They tried to think of other plans, but finally they had to accept that the three original choices, although they were hard, were the only ones the war allowed. Inman could not accept the first suggestion. Ada felt that the second was too dangerous. So they decided on the third. Over the mountains. Three days or four of steady walking, and then he would cross into the next state, put up his hands, and say that the South had been beaten.

In the end, they both promised to keep in their minds Inman's return home in three or four months' time. They would go forward from there into whatever new world the war left behind. And they would do their best to create the future that they had imagined in their talks two nights ago.

♦

On the fourth day in the village, brown leaves and black dirt started to appear on the ground. That day Stobrod could sit up without support and they could mostly understand what he said. His wounds were clean and he could eat solid food. By the fifth day, the snow was more than half gone and Stobrod announced that he was ready to travel.

"Six hours home," Ruby said. "Seven at most."

Ada thought that they would all go as a group, but Inman would not allow it.

"Why put everyone in danger, when it's us they want," he said, pointing in Stobrod's direction.

He suggested that Ruby and Ada walk on ahead while he and Stobrod followed a short way behind, with Stobrod on the horse. They would wait in the woods until dark. The next morning, he would start on his journey into the next state. The women would keep Stobrod hidden at home, and if the war had not ended by the time he had healed, they would send him across the mountains to join Inman.

Stobrod had no opinion on the matter, but Ruby agreed with Inman, so that is what they did. The women started walking, and Inman stood and watched them climb the hillside. When Ada disappeared into the trees, a part of the richness of the world seemed to go with her. He had been alone in the world and empty for so long. But she filled him full, and he believed that perhaps everything that had been taken out of him had been for a purpose. To clear space for something better.

He waited for a time and then put Stobrod on the horse and followed, passing Pangle's grave, still covered with snow. They traveled for some distance, dark clouds floating above them, the path rough and steep. Then they heard sounds behind them and turned to see horsemen on the path.

"Good God," Stobrod said.

Teague said, "That's a hard man to kill."

Stobrod looked at the men and recognized Teague and the boy he kept at his side. The other three men he did not know.

Inman looked around to see what protection there was. He wanted a stone wall, but there was none. He studied the Guards and he knew them by the look in their eye. There was no point in talking with such men. Language would change nothing. He hit the horse hard with his left hand and pulled out his pistol with his right, shooting one of the men in a single movement. Stobrod's horse went running down the path and disappeared into the trees.

There was a moment of stillness, and then a great deal of movement. The horses all jumped and the riders pulled at their heads to calm them down. Inman ran straight at the group. There was no wall to get behind, no hope to do anything except run into them and try to kill them all.

He shot one rider off his horse. That left only three, and one was already moving away toward the trees. Inman fired again and a horse came down, falling on the leg of one of the riders, who shouted in pain. The other horse started spinning out of control and Teague almost came off. Inman ran to him and pulled the gun from his hand.

The two men looked each other in the eyes, and Teague pulled out a long knife and shouted, "I'll blacken my knife with your blood."

Inman fired and the bullet hit Teague in the chest. He fell to the ground, screaming and swearing. Inman hit him on the side of the head with his gun and the man stopped screaming.

Inman looked around for the last rider. He expected the man to have run away, but he found him about fifty meters away, hiding behind a tree. Inman saw that he was only a boy and that he had lost his hat. His head was white. He probably had German or Dutch blood in him, but he was now American, white skin, white hair, and a killer. He looked very young and Inman did not want to shoot a boy.

"Come out of there," Inman said, making his voice loud enough to be heard.

Nothing. The boy stayed behind the tree.

"Come on," Inman said. "I'm not asking again. Put down your gun and you can ride home."

"No, sir," the boy said. "Here's fine."

"Listen," Inman said. "I'm looking for a way not to kill you."

"And I'm looking for a way to finish you," said the boy.

Inman pointed his gun at the tree. "You're going to have to come out from behind that tree sometime," he said.

The boy and his horse rode off through the woods and Inman went after him. They chased each other, using the trees to hide behind, and the horse became confused and started jumping around, throwing the boy off her. He lay in the snow where he had fallen. Then he half sat and put his hand to his gun.

"Put that thing down," Inman said. He had his gun pointed at the boy.

The boy looked at him and his blue eyes were empty as ice. He looked white in the face, a little blond thing, his hair cut close to his head. Only his hand moved, and it moved quicker than you could see.

Inman suddenly lay on the ground.

The boy sat and looked at him and then looked at the pistol in his hand.

♦

Ada heard the gunshots in the distance, dry and thin as sticks breaking. She did not say anything to Ruby. She just turned and ran. Her hat flew off her head and she kept running and left it on the ground like a shadow behind her. She met Stobrod, holding tight onto his horse.

"Back there," Stobrod said.

When she reached the place, the boy had already gathered the horses and gone. She went to the men on the ground and looked at them, and then she found Inman lying apart from them. She sat and held him in her lap. He tried to talk, but she silenced him. He floated in and out of a bright dream of home. It had a stream rising out of rock, black dirt fields, old trees. In his dream the year seemed to be happening all at one time, all the seasons coming together. Apple trees heavy with fruit and flowers, ice around the stream, red fall leaves floating down on summer roses.

From a distance it looked like a charming scene in the winter woods. A stream, a pair of lovers. The man lying with his head in the woman's lap. She looking down into his eyes, stroking his hair. He putting an arm around the softness of her body. Both touching each other with great closeness. A scene of such quiet and peace that the observer could imagine that long years of happy union stretched ahead of the two on the ground.

Chapter 13   October, 1874

Even after all this time and three children together, Ada still found them holding each other at the strangest moments. Earlier that day it had been out in the potato field. They had stood, their legs wide, each with one arm around the other, the other hand on their shovels. Ada had found them standing there, and had wanted to make a comment but had said nothing.

The Georgia boy had never gone back home, and had become a man in Black Cove. Ruby had kept him working hard for two years and she did not stop when he became her husband. His name was Reid. Their babies had been born eighteen months apart, all boys, with thick black hair and shiny brown eyes. They were growing into short, strong boys with pink cheeks and happy smiles, and Ruby made them work hard and play hard.

Now, late in the afternoon, the three boys sat around a fire behind the house. Four small chickens were roasting over the fire as the boys argued about who should turn them.

Ada watched them as she spread a cloth on the small table under the apple tree, and placed eight plates on it. October, 1874 was as fine as the month can be in the mountains. It had been dry and warm and clear for weeks, and the leaves were half red and half green. The color of Cold Mountain behind the house changed each day, and if you watched closely, you could follow the red as it came down the mountain and spread into the cove like a wave breaking over you slowly.

Soon, with an hour of daylight left, Ruby came out from the kitchen. At her side was a tall girl of nine, both of them carrying baskets of potato salad, corn, corn bread, green beans. Reid took the chickens from the fire and Ruby and the girl spread the food on the table. Stobrod came and put a bucket of milk by the table. They all took their places.

Later, as the sun was setting, Stobrod took out his fiddle and played, while the children ran around the fire and shouted. They were not dancing but just running to the music, and the girl waved a burning stick until Ada told her to stop it.

The girl said, "But Mama," and Ada shook her head. The girl came and kissed her cheek and danced away and threw the stick into the flames.

When Stobrod at last stopped playing, the children sat down by the fire. Ada took a book and began to read them a story. She turned the pages with slight difficulty because she had lost the end of the first finger on her right hand four years previously. She had been up on the hill cutting trees and had by accident taken her fingertip off. Ruby had cared for it, and a year later it had healed so well that you hardly noticed the difference.

When Ada reached the end of the story, the night was growing cool and she put the book away. The children were sleepy, and morning would come as early and demanding as always. It was time to put out the fire and go inside and lock the door.

ACTIVITIES

Chapters 1–2

Before you read

1 Look at the Word List at the back of this book. Which of the words refer to:

  a types of food?

  b features of the natural world?

  c forms of transport?

2 Read the Introduction at the start of the novel and answer these questions.

  a When was the American Civil War?

  b What do you think might happen to Inman as he tries to return home?

  c Who do you think Ada is? Why doesn't she recognize Inman?

While you read

3 Who:

  a owns a farm that has grown wild? ....

  b has a friend called Swimmer? ....

  c offers to help on a farm? ....

  d drinks coffee in town? ....

  e wakes at dawn in the hospital? ....

  f falls asleep in the woods? ....

  g leaves the hospital? ....

  h is attacked by a rooster? ....

  i visits the grave of his/her father? ....

  j has a wound in the neck? ....

  k was a preacher? ....

After you read

4 List what you have learned about these subjects.

  a Inman's childhood   **e** the Home Guard

  b Inman's wound   **f** Ruby

  c Swimmer   **g** Cold Mountain and the

  d Monroe's death   people who live there

5 Describe Inman's feelings about the war and what it has done to him.

6 Work with a partner. Act out the conversation that Ada might have with Mrs. Swanger about her problems and the choices she must make. Imagine that she has this conversation before she meets Ruby.

Chapters 3–5

Before you read

7 Discuss these questions. Give reasons for your answers.

  a Why do you think Inman leaves the hospital in the middle of the night? What does he plan to do?

  b What do you think the relationship might be between Inman and Ada? Give reasons for your answers.

  c How do you think the relationship between Ada and Ruby will develop?

While you read

8 Are these sentences true (T) or false (F)?

  a Inman is attacked by two men.   .....

  b Inman goes to church to see Sally Swanger.   .....

  c Inman rescues a woman from a preacher.   .....

  d Ada falls into Inman's lap in church.   .....

  e Stobrod Thewes is a good father.   .....

  f Junior uses his wife and her sisters to trap deserters.   .....

  g The Guards kill all their prisoners.   .....

  h A slave hides Inman and feeds him.   .....

After you read

9 At the end of Chapter 5 we learn that "Inman feared that all men shared the same nature." What do you think this means? List the bad things that have happened to Inman in these chapters to make him feel this.

10 Describe the character of each of the following people. Give reasons for your opinions:

Inman   Ada   Ruby

11 Describe how the relationship between Inman and Ada develops in these chapters.

Chapters 6–7

Before you read

12 Do you think Inman will succeed in returning home safely? What other good or bad things could happen to him on the way?

While you read

13 Circle the correct ending to each sentence.

    a The women from Tennessee are escaping from
       the Federals.   the Home Guard.

    b Ada and Ruby go to town and
       meet some friends.   do some shopping.

    c The prisoner tells the crowd how the Guards
       shot and wounded him.   killed his father and two outliers.

    d Inman meets an old woman who keeps
       goats.   pigs.

    e The Federals who rob Sara's home
       kill her pig.   steal her pig.

    f Inman kills
       the Federals.   the Federals and their horses.

After you read

14 Answer these questions.

    a How do Ada and Ruby help the women from Tennessee?

    b Why is the prisoner who talks to the crowd so angry?

    c What is unusual about the goatwoman?

    d Why is life so difficult for Sara?

    e How does Inman help Sara?

    f How does Inman feel about himself after the events in these chapters?

15 Work with a partner. Discuss these questions: What are your feelings about Inman now? Have his actions changed your opinion of him?

Chapters 8–9

Before you read

16 Discuss these questions. If Inman gets back home safely,

   a what problems might he have?

   b how might life be difficult for him?

While you read

17 Complete each sentence with a suitable word.

   a Inman tells Ada a Cherokee Indian story about the Shining
      ....

   b Ada goes to town because she wants to visit ....

   c Stobrod is living in a .... in the mountains.

   d Stobrod and Pangle both play the ....

   e At first, Ruby refuses to .... Stobrod.

   f Pangle tells the Guards where the .... is.

   g The Guards put Stobrod and Pangle against a tree and
      .... them.

   h The .... from Georgia tells Ruby and Ada what
      happened to Stobrod and Pangle.

   i The women find Pangle and .... him.

   j The women carry Stobrod to an old Cherokee ....

18 Who is speaking? What are they talking about?

   a "That was a strange story. You don't believe it, do you?"

   b "I'll see you when I see you."

   c "I didn't follow my heart. I'm sorry for that."

   d "My daddy's out on the porch."

   e "The problem is, I need help. I'm frightened."

   f "We're looking for a group of outliers living in a cave."

   g "I can't shoot a man who's smiling at me."

   h "I saw it all, saw it all."

   i "It's too far home. He won't get there alive."

19 Work in pairs. Act out the conversation between the Georgia boy
and Ruby, when the boy arrives at Black Cove.

Chapters 10–13

Before you read

20 Look at the titles of Chapters 10–13 on the Contents page. How do you think the story will end?

While you read

21 Write yes or no in answer to these questions.

    a Does Inman find Ada when he first visits Black Cove? .....

    b Is Inman able to follow the women's tracks to the Cherokee village? .....

    c Does Ada succeed in shooting a wild turkey? .....

    d Does Ada recognize Inman immediately? .....

    e Do Inman and Ada talk about their feelings for each other? .....

    f Do they decide that Inman should stay and hide in Black Cove? .....

    g Does Inman save Stobrod's life? .....

    h Does Inman kill Teague? .....

    i Does Inman kill Birch? .....

    j Does the Georgia boy return to Georgia? .....

    k Does Ada have Inman's child? .....

After you read

22 List the topics that Inman and Ada talk about when they are finally together.

23 Work with a partner. Discuss these questions. Give reasons for your opinion.

    a How do you feel about the fact that Inman dies?

    b Would you describe Inman as a good man?

    c If Inman had lived, do you think he would have been able to return to a normal life?

    d How do you think Ada feels about her life and what has happened to her, in the final chapter?

Writing

24 Write one or two paragraphs about each of Ada, Stobrod, and Ruby, describing how their lives change and how they themselves change.

25 What is the deeper meaning of Cold Mountain and the Shining Rocks in the novel? What do they mean to Inman, and why does he intend to go to the Shining Rocks if Ada will not have him?

26 Discuss this statement: *Cold Mountain* explores war and its effect on human nature.

27 Write about *Cold Mountain* for a magazine. Write a short description of the story and state your opinion of the novel.

28 Write two short descriptions of Ada from the point of view of Ruby, one at the beginning and one at the end of the book.

29 Write a letter from Ada to her cousin Lucy in Charleston, describing her life in Black Cove with her daughter, and with Ruby and her family.

Answers for the Activities in this book are available from the Penguin Readers website:
www.penguinreaders.com
A free Factsheet for this book is also available from this website.